"You're early," she said.

Confusion crossed his features. *Adorable.* Oh yes! He was hired before he even got inside her office. He was tall and toned with clean-cut features. It was hard to find an attractive male model without a beard these days. And those bright blue eyes were going to light up her camera.

"I try to always be on time, if not early," he said.

He came inside, shifting the box. "Where do you want this?" he asked.

"What is it?"

"It's an Apple computer. But I think it's supposed to be a surprise."

"Just set it here, on the floor," she said, indicating the space beside her desk. The relief was evident on his face as he set it down. Danielle didn't see a card attached.

"Sit," she said, nodding toward the empty chair in front of her desk.

After he sat, she laced her fingers under her chin and allowed herself to gaze into his eyes. "How long have you been a model?" She asked.

"I'm not a model."

She smiled as she considered the possibility of exclusivity. She could be the only graphic artist with his handsome face on book covers. "So... no experience?"

He frowned and shook his head. "Not with modeling."

"It's okay," she said quickly. "You don't have to have experience."

He grinned and leaned back in his chair.

Okay, maybe he's a little too relaxed.

"Maybe we could--" Her phone buzzed. It was a text from her father.

Is Samuel there yet?

She wrote back. *Who is Samuel?*

I sent him to bring your birthday present.

Danielle looked up at the man sitting across from her. Her hopes for exclusivity crumbled.

Is it a computer? She texted.

Silence.

"Are you Samuel?" she asked, looking up at the man sitting across from her.

He nodded.

Danielle scowled at her phone. *Who is Samuel?* She typed again.

My newest pilot.

She glared at Samuel, who wasn't smiling anymore. "You're a pilot," she said, unable to keep the accusation out of her voice.

"Right now I wish I wasn't," he said, straightening in his chair, one hand on the chair arm.

FALLING AGAIN

ALSO BY KATHRYN KALEIGH

Contemporary Romance
The Worthington Family

The Heart of Christmas

The Magic of Christmas

Second Chance Kisses

Second Chance Secrets

First Time Charm

Three Broken Rules

Second Chance Destiny

Unexpected Vows

Billionaire's Unexpected Landing

Billionaire's Accidental Girlfriend

Billionaire Fallen Angel

Begin Again

Love Again

Falling Again

Just Stay

Just Chance

Just Believe

Just Us

Just Once

Just Happened

Just Maybe

Just Pretend

Just Because

FALLING AGAIN

THE WORTHINGTONS

KATHRYN KALEIGH

FALLING AGAIN

PREVIEW: JUST STAY

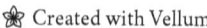

To learn more about Kathryn Kaleigh, visit

www.kathrynkaleigh.com

Kathryn Kaleigh

1

*A*t the moment, Danielle Worthington was having a hard time believing in true love, much less happily ever after.

After unclipping the camera from the tripod, she adjusted the camera's shutter speed and photographed the models in front of her. The models were *posing* as a happy couple. They wore jeans and t-shirts to portray a casual, relaxed look, and stood in front of an historic wooden house with a white picket fence at Sam Houston Park.

They were depicting the American Dream.

Their smiles looked true and their affection genuine, but Avery and Jacob could barely stand the sight of each other.

Jacob put his arm around Avery and pulled her close. They gazed at each other, their faces only inches apart. Danielle went up the stairs and stood on the other side of them. She took more photos. They were such a cute couple.

"I've got enough casual," Danielle said. "Go get dressed up, guys."

As Jacob and Avery turned away from each other, their

smiles turned to scowls. At least they were professional enough to pretend to like each other during the shoots.

Danielle glanced at her phone. She had two hours to get back to her office in time to meet her father for lunch. A wave of anxiety swept over her in anticipation of that meeting.

She took a deep breath and swallowed the nausea. Her father loved her no matter what. *Right?*

He'd always been there for her. There was no reason why he wouldn't be there for her now.

Avery and Jacob were back within minutes. Avery was now wearing a red party dress, and Jacob was wearing a black tux.

They made such a beautiful couple.

Danielle's heart did a little summersault as an image of *that* night flashed through her mind. The night that she had worn a floor-length red dress, and Joey had worn a black suit. Danielle had felt like a princess that night. She'd thought they were in a fairy tale.

The fairy tale hadn't collapsed at midnight, but at six a.m. the next morning. That girl, whatever her name was, had been surprised that Joey wasn't alone. In fact, that was the only satisfaction that Danielle took from the whole fiasco.

Now she saw her relationship with Joey for what it had been all along: a sham, just like Avery and Jacob. She'd fallen for an illusion.

Never again.

After taking several more photos, she could tell that they were getting tired, and she needed to rest too.

Walking back to the parking lot, she enjoyed the warmth of the Houston sun. She'd lived here for six weeks now, but already she had found that she liked the friendliness of the people and the warmth of the weather.

A Los Angeles native, Houston wouldn't have been her first choice. She had an affinity for New York, though she'd only visited there once with her stepmother, Savannah, whose love for the big city had been contagious.

Nonetheless, Danielle was content with Houston.

Except for one small detail.

When she got to the parking lot, she had to call an Uber. Houston was definitely a driving town, and Danielle would be content if she never had to drive.

After the Uber driver picked her up, she noticed an American flag decal on his rearview mirror. Seeing it was like taking an instant punch to the gut.

Her ex-boyfriend, ex of five weeks and four days, was in the Air Force, stationed here in Houston. They'd been on-again-off-again for several years. When he'd suggested she move to Houston, she'd thought they were moving forward. Together.

Unfortunately, she'd been moving forward alone. Danielle had subsequently implemented a self-imposed dating moratorium. It hadn't been hard to do since she was in a strange town and knew absolutely no one other than coworkers. And since they all worked independently, she really didn't know them either.

She'd found a furnished apartment to rent, a job, and left home for the first time.

Okay, she admitted to herself that there were other factors involved. One, her mother had just gotten married a second time, this time to her high school sweetheart, so moving out of the house was long overdue. And second, Houston put her a little closer to her father, who lived in Alabama and had a charter flight company in Fort Worth.

Though she hadn't seen him in nearly two months, he was flying down today to take her to lunch for her birthday. Today, she would tell him that she and Joey had broken up, and she was living alone in Houston. And again, the thought made her queasy. Odd. She'd never been nervous about seeing her father before.

Maybe she'd picked up a virus.

*S*amuel Johnson was not a shopper by nature. In fact, he considered himself a man of very minimal needs: basic clothing, an iPhone and iPad, a uniform for work, and a reliable truck. Oh, and an airplane. In fact, the airplane was first on his list, but it was such a basic thing, he rarely even thought about it. Sort of like air.

As a result, standing in the Apple store in Highland Shopping Center trying to decide whether to buy an iMac, a MacBook, a MacBook Air, or a MacBook Pro had him so completely out of his element, that he couldn't process.

Get her a good Apple computer and put it on the company credit card. What the boss requested, the boss got.

Especially when the boss was Noah Worthington of Skye Travels. The man who was paying him for two weeks *before* he even started work to give him time to relocate from Houston to Dallas.

The store wasn't busy this morning, and Tom, one of the blue-shirted employees, stood patiently waiting while Samuel considered his options.

"Do you have any questions?" Tom asked.

Samuel nodded. "Which one should I get?"

Tom laughed. "What do you need it for?"

"I have no idea."

"No problem," Tom assured him.

"It's not for me. It's for... my boss's daughter."

"Ah." Tom's eyes widened knowingly. "What kind of work does she do?"

"I have absolutely no clue."

"Oh boy."

"Yeah. Oh boy indeed." He knew her name and the fact that her father was a pilot and owner of Skye Travels, so she couldn't be very old. "I know today's her birthday."

"Well, if she works at a desk, you should probably go with the iMac. If she travels, you can't go wrong with any of the notebooks."

"Her father's a pilot."

"Too bad it's not for him." Tom scratched his chin. "Can you ask him?"

Samuel glanced at his watch. "Not likely. He should be in the air."

"I don't suppose you could ask her?"

Samuel shook his head. "Not even a chance. It's a surprise."

"We have a fourteen-day return policy."

A ray of hope opened up, and it was as though the weight of the world fell from Samuel's shoulders. "Which one is more expensive?"

"The MacBook Pro."

Samuel tapped the keys on the notebook computer. But the images on the MacBook Pro drew his attention. "I like that one," he said more to himself than to Tom.

"It's a great computer. It just came out."

Samuel glanced at his watch. *Always go with your gut.* He

knew not to overthink things. *Go with your first reaction unless you have compelling evidence not to.* The wisdom drilled into him as a pilot never failed to spill over into other parts of his life. Besides, if he didn't make a decision and get moving, he was going to be late.

3
_____

Two hours later, Danielle looked up from her computer at a knock on her open door. A man holding a large box, half as tall as he was, stood in her doorway.

He wasn't wearing a uniform, so he didn't appear to be a delivery guy. Besides, the box was wrapped in what at first glance appeared to be blue birthday wrapping paper, not shipping paper.

A birthday gift? No one here at the office knew it was her birthday.

She glanced at the time on her computer. She had a male model coming in to interview at three o'clock. Maybe he was early. She could get that out of the way while she waited on her father who was characteristically late. No doubt he would blame it on the weather or other flight delay problems.

"You're early," she said.

Confusion crossed his features. *Adorable*. Oh yes! He was hired before he even got inside her office. He was tall and toned with clean-cut features. It was hard to find an attractive male model without a beard these days. And those bright blue eyes were going to light up her camera.

"I try to always be on time, if not early," he said.

Too bad she wasn't doing audio. His smooth voice would be perfect.

"Come in," she said. "I'm meeting someone, but he's late. We can go ahead."

He came inside, shifting the box. "Where do you want this?" he asked.

"What is it?"

"It's an Apple computer. But I think it's supposed to be a surprise."

Danielle glanced at the smaller Apple computer sitting on her desk and salivated just a little.

Who all knew she wanted a new, larger, computer? Her mother, Claire, her father, Noah, and her ex-boyfriend.

"Just set it here, on the floor," she said, indicating the space beside her desk. The relief was evident on his face as he set it down. Danielle didn't see a card attached.

I'll have to come back to this.

"Sit," she said, nodding toward the empty chair in front of her desk.

After he sat, she laced her fingers under her chin and allowed herself to gaze into his eyes. "How long have you been a model?" She asked.

"I'm not a model."

She smiled as she considered the possibility of exclusivity. She could be the only graphic artist with his handsome face on book covers. "So... no experience?"

He frowned and shook his head. "Not with modeling."

"It's okay," she said quickly. "You don't have to have experience."

He grinned and leaned back in his chair.

Okay, maybe he's a little too relaxed.

"Maybe we could--" Her phone buzzed. It was a text from her father.

Is Samuel there yet?

She wrote back. *Who is Samuel?*

I sent him to bring your birthday present.

Danielle looked up at the man sitting across from her. Her hopes for exclusivity crumbled.

Is it a computer? She texted.

Silence.

"Are you Samuel?" she asked, looking up at the man sitting across from her.

He nodded.

Where are you? She texted.

Stuck at the airport in Dallas. Thunderstorms.

"When was he going to tell me that?" She asked, rolling her eyes.

"I'm not sure," Samuel said.

Danielle scowled at her phone. *Who is Samuel?* She typed again.

My newest pilot.

Why is he here?

In the process of moving. I took advantage of him being in Houston.

Danielle blew her bangs out of her eyes and ran a hand through her hair.

She glared at Samuel, who wasn't smiling anymore. "You're a pilot," she said, unable to keep the accusation out of her voice.

"Right now I wish I wasn't," he said, straightening in his chair, one hand on the chair arm. "I can go," he said.

Don't go. "Wait," she said.

He sat back, watching her expectantly.

"You work for my father." She made sure to keep her voice calm.

"I started yesterday. Today, he sent me to buy your birthday present."

She smiled. "That's my father." She glanced at the box in her floor. "Who wrapped it?"

"I did," he said.

"That seems like a lot to ask."

"Oh," Samuel said. "He didn't ask me to wrap it. He just asked me to pick it up from the Apple store and drop it off here. He said he didn't have time to pick it up before he met you for lunch."

She melted a little at the thought of this man – this handsome stranger – picking up wrapping paper for her gift and wrapping the computer himself.

"He's not coming," she said.

"It's storming in Dallas," he said.

"Yeah," she said, checking her phone. No messages. She shoved it aside.

"Do you have alternate plans for your birthday lunch?" he asked.

She sighed. "I'll just order something and have it delivered. I might use the time to set up this computer."

"I can take you to lunch."

Her eyes widened. The old Danielle Worthington would have jumped at the opportunity to have lunch with a pilot who looked like a model.

No. The new Danielle was under a dating moratorium. *Maybe I should go to AA. Hi, I'm Danielle. I haven't had a date in five weeks, four days, and ten hours.*

Lunch technically wasn't a date.

I'm Danielle. Please help me.

He was waiting for an answer.

"I'm--" *I'm normally not this daft.* "I can't," she said.

He was frowning again. "But... it's your birthday. Surely you want company."

"I do, but--" *You're too tempting.*

The wave of nausea came out of the blue. It lodged in the

back of her throat, and she knew without a doubt that she was going to be sick. She held up a hand. "I'm going to be sick," she said. *I should not have skipped breakfast.*

She slipped out of her chair onto her knees and, turning her head just in time, threw up into the wastebasket.

As she hunched over the wastebasket, gagging, she felt Samuel pull her hair back and hold it. He handed her a Kleenex, and she wiped her mouth.

It was one of the most mortifying things she'd ever had happen. So much for impressing the handsome pilot – that she would not, absolutely would not, go out with. Or even out to lunch.

"Thank you," she said. "I'm better now."

He put a hand under her elbow to help her up. After she was safely back in her chair, he placed a hand on her forehead. "No fever."

"You're a doctor now?" She asked.

"No, but when I was five-years-old, my mother decided to give me two little sisters."

"Wow. I don't envy either one of you."

"You don't like children?" He asked, pulling the plastic bag from her trash can and tying it up.

"They're okay. Just not for me."

"I'll be right back," he said, leaving the room and taking the plastic bag with him.

Danielle leaned back and closed her eyes – just for a moment. Then she pulled a mirror out of her handbag and quickly checked her appearance.

This was not good. First of all, she was rarely sick. But that wave of nausea had been overwhelming. This was November. Was there a bug going around? She'd felt okay... Then she remembered the nausea this morning while they were shooting. She was definitely coming down with something.

And second, it was not cool to throw up in front of a hot

model pilot. Even if she wasn't dating right now, and she wasn't, she could not be throwing up in front of him and having him hold her hair.

She groaned. And sighed. He'd held her hair.

And checked her for fever.

It was good thing she wasn't open to dating.

Samuel came back into the room and placed a package of saltine crackers on the desk in front of her as he sat back down in the chair.

"What?" She asked.

"They're good for nausea," he explained. When she just looked at him, he reached over, opened the package and held it up for her.

She pulled a cracker from the sleeve. "Where did you get these?"

He shrugged. "My truck." He set the crackers back on her desk.

Danielle nibbled the end off the cracker. "You keep crackers in your truck?"

"My mom has me keep some with me in case I forget to eat."

Danielle finished the cracker and reached for another one. She swallowed a bubble of laughter. He was a mama's boy. It was cute.

"Your mother's pretty smart. I feel better."

"Good." He grinned. "Let's go get something to eat, then we can get this computer set up."

"But…"

He shook his head. "There's no way I'm leaving you now. You don't get to throw up on your birthday, then eat by yourself."

He must think she was pathetic. "I had plans."

"Yes, I know. Your dad. But he can't be here right now." Samuel lifted an eyebrow and smiled at her. "And since I work for him, I'm your alternate lunch escort."

It's not a date. It's an alternate lunch escort. He was right. She did need to eat. And it was kind of pathetic to be eating lunch alone on her birthday.

She wasn't going to tell him that her plan for tonight was to have pizza delivered to her apartment. Alone.

4

---

*S*amuel Johnson was not impulsive.

He also hadn't dated anyone since Jessica, his girlfriend of four years, had been killed in Afghanistan two years ago. So for two years, he'd kept his heart guarded.

At twenty-five, he wasn't easily impressed. He kept his head down and his heart in the sky. As a pilot, the only place he felt at peace was in the air. That's where he felt closest to Jessica. With Jessica in Heaven, it was his way of staying close to her.

Ironically, his focus on flying these last two years had given him a marketable edge. He hadn't planned on ever leaving Houston, but when he was filling out applications, he'd run across an ad for Skye Travels. He wasn't sure why Noah Worthington even advertised. His company was legendary.

When Noah had called him to interview and then offered him a job on the spot, Samuel had hesitated. He'd put Noah off for two weeks. He was pretty sure that no one ever put Noah Worthington off, certainly not for two weeks.

But in the end, he couldn't resist the offer to work for Noah, even if it meant leaving Houston. Technically, he was already on the payroll. He had to take one flight up to Dallas to meet with Noah this week, but otherwise, he'd spend the week packing and getting everything ready to move. Not a bad way to spend the first week on the job.

Until this morning. This morning, Noah had called and asked him to not only pick up a birthday present for his daughter, who just happened to live in Houston, but also to deliver it to her.

Samuel found the whole thing a little perplexing. There was no way that Noah Worthington thought he was going to fly out of Dallas today. Legend had it that Noah was better at forecasting than most meteorologists.

He was also well-known for his stubbornness. Samuel supposed that his daughter's birthday wasn't something he would give up lightly. If there had been a way for him to get here, Samuel had little doubt that he would have done so.

Samuel had been surprised to learn that Noah had a daughter living in Houston. He had heard that he had an ex-wife living in California and a current wife living in Alabama. Samuel hadn't paid much attention to whether or not he had children.

He had a daughter all right. Samuel was nearly speechless as he watched Danielle gingerly nibbling on a cracker. She was beautiful, and he could most definitely see where she could be from California. Her long hair was a swirl of pale lavender and brunette. And it was soft. When he'd held her hair back while she was throwing up, he'd been in awe at the softness of it.

If he hadn't known better, he would have thought she was pregnant. He almost laughed out loud at the idea. That definitely didn't fit his first impression. She'd even suggested she didn't want children.

"Are you better?" He asked.

She nodded and gave him a half-smile. It was the same expression he'd seen on Noah's face.

"Good."

"I'm so sorry." She swept her hair up and dropped it across her left shoulder. "I feel mortified."

"No need to apologize." He kept his gaze on her mesmerizing green eyes. "Remember. Two little sisters."

"Maybe so, but I'm not your sister."

Thank goodness for that. It had been a long time since Samuel had been this attracted to anyone. About six years, to be precise. He remembered the day he'd met Jessica like it was yesterday. Jessica was nothing like Danielle. Jessica had been jogging in Houston Park with no makeup and her natural-brown hair pulled back in a ponytail. She'd been friendly.

Samuel had been playing Frisbee with his golden retriever, Jack, when the Frisbee landed right at Jessica's feet. Samuel had always thought it was divine intervention. Laughing, she'd picked it up, and tossed it back toward Samuel. Jack had stopped to look at her, barked once, then turned around and went after the Frisbee.

"Thanks," Samuel had called out as she waved and jogged away. Three days later, Samuel and Jack had been sitting on a park bench waiting for her. When she saw them, she stopped right in front of them and bent over, hands on her knees, as she caught her breath.

"We're not stalking you," he'd said.

"I'm not worried," she said. "I'm lethal with my hands."

"I can't stop thinking about you."

She'd laughed. And that had been that. They had dated for two years. Then Samuel had proposed, and they'd been engaged when she was deployed to Afghanistan.

Samuel had done everything by the book. He'd had his life with Jessica planned out.

Only Jessica had been returned to him in the belly of a plane, a flag draped over her coffin.

Samuel had done little more than go through the motions for the next two years. He'd all but shut down his life, everything but flying. He stayed in the air as much as possible. When he was flying, he didn't have to worry about the world.

Or other people.

Jessica had been practical and no-nonsense. Down to earth. He never knew if the military did that to her, or if she was drawn to the military as a result of her personality. Maybe it was a little bit of both.

Now he was sitting here in front of a girl who appeared to be the exact opposite of Jessica. A girl with lavender streaks in her hair. A girl wearing perfect makeup, skinny tights, and a dark gray sweater dress.

And in the mere minutes since he'd met her, she'd thrown up in her wastebasket. Not exactly a very romantic start.

Nonetheless, Samuel was enchanted.

5

*S*amuel stood up and waited while Danielle gathered up her handbag and logged out of her computer. "Pappa's Burgers is just down the street," she said, almost salivating as she craved a shrimp po'boy. No need to tell Samuel that she had eaten lunch there every day for the last two weeks. "Can you drive?"

"Sure," he said, following her out of her office.

There was also no need to tell him that she didn't have a car. There was a city bus stop on the corner near her office. The bus stopped just walking distance from Pappa's Burgers.

As he fell into step beside her as they walked through the open lobby to the elevator, she couldn't help but notice that he was a head taller than she was. He was a good height for her. Not that she was interested.

The dating moratorium was firmly in place.

They got into the elevator and went down from the fourth floor to the first. He held the door for her as they walked through the almost-deserted first-floor lobby to the front door. The security guard nodded as they walked past.

When they got to the parking lot, she followed him to a

charcoal gray Toyota Tacoma pickup truck. Danielle smiled to herself. One thing she'd learned a long time ago. True Texas boys drove pickup trucks. He held the door as she climbed inside.

Samuel's truck smelled new and was spotless inside. He went around and got into the driver's seat. "Pappa's Burgers, right?" He asked, giving her a smile that sent tingles down to her toes.

"Yes," she said. "Do you know it?"

"Are you kidding?" He asked as he pulled onto Westheimer Road. "It's a Sunday tradition in my family."

"Seriously?"

"Yeah. My parents, my brother and his wife, my sister and her husband, my youngest sister, and both sets of my grandparents eat there for Sunday lunch all the time."

"That is so special. I'm jealous. My dad and his family live in Alabama, and my mom and her family live in California, so I don't think my entire extended family has ever been in the same restaurant at the same time."

"How sad," he said.

"Yeah," Danielle agreed, feeling her eyes tear up. It was odd, because it had never bothered her before. It was just life as she knew it.

They pulled into the little parking lot, and before he jumped out, Samuel glanced at her and said, "wait here."

He came around and opened her door. Then he held his hand out to help her climb down from the cab. She put her hand in his, and he latched on to steady her. Her eyes met his ocean blue ones, and she forgot she was supposed to be moving. Her hand felt small in his, and a sensation of being in safe hands washed over her.

She swallowed, and with a slight tug on her hand, he guided her from the truck.

When her feet were on the ground, he released her hand. *This is not good. It's not a date. He's a lunch escort.*

They went inside and stood in line to place their order. It wasn't crowded today. There were only three people ahead of them.

"I'll be right back," Danielle said, dashing toward the restroom. *I must have been drinking too much water lately.* After washing her hands, she put on some clear lip gloss and ran a hand through her hair. The colorist at Visible Changes had gotten her hair exactly right, brunette with a few tasteful purple highlights woven throughout. They'd called it a mermaid balayage. It was Danielle's first time to have hand-painted highlights, and she absolutely loved it.

By the time she got back to Samuel, he was waiting at the counter to order. The guy behind the counter smiled. "A shrimp po'boy with coleslaw?" He asked.

Samuel glanced at the menu on the wall. "That's not on the menu," he pointed out.

"It's okay," she said, feeling her cheeks flush that the guy had remembered what she'd ordered every day for the last two weeks. "They make it for me anyway."

"Huh," he said. "Make that two," he told the checker.

They got their sodas and found a booth near the back, next to the windows.

"How long have you lived in Houston?" He asked.

"Six weeks," she said, sipping her cola. "And you?"

"My entire life."

She frowned. "How are you working for my dad in Dallas and still living in Houston?"

"Unfortunately," he said, "that's about to end. I've got about one more week before I have to move."

"Oh," she said, not bothering to keep the disappointment from her voice. Despite her dating moratorium, she could still enjoy his company. Samuel seemed like someone she wanted to keep close.

"The real question is," he said, narrowing his eyes. "With your mother in California and your father in Dallas, how did you end up in Houston?"

That was a door she didn't want to walk through. She decided to stall a bit before answering. "My dad actually lives in Alabama with his second wife Savannah."

"I know," Samuel said. "But still, he has a business in Dallas – or technically Fort Worth – either way, they aren't here."

"Yeah," she said, biting her lip. "That's kind of a long story."

"I don't have anywhere else to be," he said, settling back in his seat, his eyes focusing on her. Danielle felt the heat rise in her cheeks again. Despite her dating moratorium, she was not immune to having a handsome man's undivided attention.

The server brought their sandwiches and French fries, giving her a moment to think about how much she wanted to reveal.

He took a bite of his po'boy. "This is really good," he said. "I think they used to have these on the menu."

"That's what they told me." She nibbled on a French fry and took a deep breath. "I'm in Houston because my boyfriend was transferred here," she said.

He narrowed his eyes and watched her.

"We broke up five weeks ago," she added, feeling a need to set that straight. She didn't want Samuel to think she had a boyfriend. Not that it mattered either way, she reminded herself. Was that relief she saw flicker across his features?

"Wait. You've lived here for six weeks, and you broke up five weeks ago?

"Technically five weeks and four days ago."

She could see him doing the math in his head, but he let it go. "You moved from California?"

She nodded.

"That must be quite a change."

"It's a huge change," she admitted, biting into her sandwich and closing her eyes. She was addicted to these things.

"Are you going to be moving back?"

"I don't know yet. I have a job here. A job I really like."

"There's a chance you might get back together with your boyfriend?" He asked.

"Ha. Never. Not a chance." Was she supposed to ask about his dating status? It was hard to know how to keep this from feeling like a date.

It already feels like a date.

"Why did you break up?"

She shook her head, shrugged, and looked into those blue eyes.

"I know it's none of my business," he said. "But you came a really long way to be with him. For what? Three days?"

"I don't know. We'd been together on and off for about five years. I thought it was going somewhere, you know. But it turns out he didn't."

"He cheated," Samuel said.

Danielle's eyes widened. "How did you know?"

"Two sisters," he said with a grin.

"Right. Two sisters."

"If you're so close to your family, why are you leaving?" It occurred to her that he might be moving because of a girlfriend. Or maybe a boyfriend.

"It's a great opportunity to work with your father. He's legendary, you know. And it's not like I have anything else going on."

"No girlfriend?" She asked, unable to resist.

He shook his head.

"A boyfriend?"

He laughed. "I'm heterosexual."

She laughed back and he stared at her. "That's good to know."

"Why is that good to know?" He asked.

"Well," she said. "You know. So I know how to talk to you. If you like boys, I don't want to ask you about girlfriends, and if you were gay, well, you know."

He laughed again.

Danielle was intrigued. Joey hadn't laughed with her in a long time, and she hadn't even realized it until this moment. In retrospect, there were so many clues that he was no longer into her.

"I'm glad we got that sorted out," Samuel said.

She smiled. "Me too."

Suddenly, she couldn't eat another bite. "I'm stuffed," she said.

"You barely ate anything," he pointed out.

"I know. I do that sometimes. I'm still a little queasy from… you know… earlier."

"Yeah," he said, finishing off his sandwich. "Are you gonna get that to go?"

She shook her head. "No thanks."

He reached over, picked up the other half of her uneaten sandwich and proceeded to eat it.

Danielle laughed.

"This is too good to go to waste," he said. "How did the checker know what you wanted to order?"

"I ordered it yesterday," she said. There was no need to tell him that she'd ordered it not only yesterday, but every day for the past two weeks.

"We'll have to get it again," he said.

Danielle sat back in her seat and squeezed her hands together under the table. This was dangerous territory. He used the word *we*. Danielle was nothing if not well-versed in the language of relationships.

She and Joey had been on and off for several years. Danielle always dated in between – during the "off periods."

This was more than an "off period." This was more of an exclamation point. *The end* to their relationship. Catching him cheating on her when she'd just moved all the way out here, alone, to be with him was more than she could take.

Hence, the moratorium on dating.

6

Samuel came from a large family with lots of traditions, and one of those traditions was that birthdays never went unnoticed and certainly no one was allowed to spend one alone.

Since Danielle was new to Houston, he was fairly certain that she didn't have plans for the evening.

"What do people do for fun in California?"

"People?" She grinned at him.

"Okay. You. What kinds of things do you do for fun in California?"

"I've spent a lot of time in museums and art galleries. My mom owns an art gallery."

"Do you go to museums because you like it or because it's expected?"

She seemed to consider. "I guess because I like it. But I'm not really sure. It's just what I do. No one's ever asked me that before."

"Really?" He sat back, stretched his arm along the back of the booth. "Let me ask a different way. If you could do anything you wanted on your birthday, what would it be?"

"I'd want to be whisked off to Disneyland to have dinner at the Magic Kingdom."

He mentally calculated the distance between Houston and Anaheim and then Houston and Orlando. "I could actually make that happen."

Only a pilot's daughter wouldn't find that statement odd. "You asked." She shrugged.

"Disney World is closer."

She laughed. "I've never been to Disney World." She sipped her soda. "Why do you ask?"

"Since you just moved here, I'm assuming you don't have plans for your birthday tonight."

"I do actually have plans."

"Oh." Good. He didn't have to rescue her. "What are you doing?"

"I'm going to have pizza delivered and binge watch *Hart of Dixie*."

"There are so many things wrong with that answer."

"You don't like pizza?"

"Of course I do. What's *Hart of Dixie*?"

"It's a series on Netflix about a New York doctor who moves to the south to practice medicine."

"I can see where you'd like that."

"Plus, I'm sure my mom and dad will call."

Samuel shook his head. "I can't let you do that."

Her eyes widened. She hadn't been shocked that he could fly her to Disney World, but she was shocked that he wouldn't let her spend her birthday alone. Nonetheless, she took it in stride. "What do you suggest then?"

"I sounds like I can either take you to Disney or a museum."

She laughed. "It'd be hard for me to go to work tomorrow after a late flight. And, to be honest, I really don't feel like going to a museum."

"What else do you like? Bowling? Sky diving? Dancing?"

"Ha. Since I had planned to have pizza delivered and watch TV, you can probably guess that I'm actually rather boring."

"I seriously doubt that."

"Well, not very adventurous either."

"Danielle, you have a tendency to sell yourself short. You picked up and moved to Houston from California without knowing anyone other than the one person you'd probably rather not think about right now."

"Yeah." She stared out the window for a minute. "I like movies." She turned back to smile at him.

Samuel grinned. "Then since you won't let me fly you to the Magic Castle, can I take you to a movie?"

7

"*I*t's not a date." Danielle rolled her eyes.

"It's okay if it is." Danielle could tell that her mother was smiling, even through the phone.

"I'm on a dating moratorium."

"Right."

"Oh and Mom." Danielle walked to her window and stared at the traffic below. "Since Dad didn't make it for lunch, I still haven't told him about breaking up with Joey."

Her mother was silent for a moment.

"Mom? Did you tell him?"

"It's not like I talk to him every day. In fact, I haven't spoken to your father in weeks."

"Good." She blew out a breath of relief. "I need to tell him myself."

"I understand. Enjoy your evening out. It's been a long time."

Danielle turned and saw Samuel getting off the elevator. "Mom. He's here. I have to go." Her pulse jumped into overtime, and she suddenly wished she'd had him pick her up at her apartment so she could have showered and changed.

Fortunately, she kept heels at the office, and she'd slipped into them. *It's not a date.*

"Happy Birthday, sweetheart."

"Love you, Mom."

Danielle closed her cell phone and slipped it into her pocket.

Samuel stopped at her door and grinned at her. He held a little gift bag in his hand. "I brought you something."

"Aw. You didn't have to do that."

"I promise. It's nothing." He handed it to her. "Nothing like the Apple computer I brought you this morning."

She took the gift bag. Her father *had* sent Samuel to buy her computer. "Hmm."

"Do you want to set it up? We have time." He nodded toward the computer, now unwrapped but still sitting on her floor.

"Okay." She reached into the gift bag and pulled out a book. *Things to do in Houston.* She looked up and laughed. She hadn't seen him take two steps toward her.

He was standing much too close. Close enough for her to gaze into his sky-blue eyes beneath soft lashes. He smelled good; clean and earthy. Sandalwood? Her gaze strayed to his kissable lips curved up at the corners in a smile.

"I… um…" She took a step back. Held the book to her chest.

"It's a welcome gift." He didn't move. "To Houston. In case you're interested in what there is to do here."

"Thank you." She swallowed, her mouth suddenly very dry.

"Do you have scissors?" He nodded toward the computer box.

Spurred into movement, she went behind her desk and opened three drawers before she found a pair of scissors. She handed them to him and watched as he slid it through the seal. She was obviously the only one affected. This was not a good thing.

"Did you decide on a movie?" He pulled the computer from its box.

She shook her head. "I've been on the phone."

After setting the computer on her desk, he pulled his phone out of his front pocket and after a couple of clicks, handed it to her. "I have an app. This theater is the one closest to us."

As she scrolled through the movies, he said. "I don't mind romantic movies." He took the plastic off the computer and plugged the cord into the back.

By the time she could focus enough to choose a movie, he had the computer set up.

"How about this one?" She handed the phone back to him.

"Looks good to me." He glanced at the screen. "We have time for dinner."

"Sure."

"Where do you want your computer?"

She'd already decided how to rearrange her desk, so she quickly pointed out where to put the computer.

"Ready?" He asked.

She grabbed her handbag and jacket. "Yep. All good."

After she locked her door, they went to the elevator and rode down in silence.

"Are you in the mood for anything in particular?" He held the elevator door while she stepped through.

"I saw a Cheesecake Factory at the Galleria."

"Cheesecake Factory it is."

He opened the door on the passenger side of the truck, and she put one foot up on the running board. Her other foot wobbled a little. This was going to be a little difficult in heels.

"Can I help?" Samuel asked, again standing near.

She laughed. "Yes. I think so." She reached out to put her hand on his arm, but he picked her up by the waist and set her on the seat. "Oh. Thanks."

He went around to the driver's side and hopped in.

"I'm not used to trucks." She wasn't sure if it was normal to have trouble climbing into the cab or not.

"It's okay. It's a Texas thing. What do you drive?"

"I don't."

He glanced doubtfully in her direction, then put his eyes back on the road.

"Help me understand."

She smiled. "I have a car in L.A., but I never drive it. To be honest, I'm not even sure what it is. It's something my father bought me. I drove him to the airport once."

"You don't drive?"

"No." She laughed.

"I've never met anyone who didn't drive."

"You have to be kidding."

"No. Maybe it's just here, but growing up, getting our driver's license and something to drive is what we all look forward to."

"Yeah. I'd rather do something else."

He pulled into the Galleria parking lot and drove up to the valet. "Like what?"

"What do I do? Make phone calls. Text messages. Read. Anything."

He got out of the truck, shaking his head. "I'll come around."

The valet already had her door open, but Samuel stepped to her, put his hands on her waist, and set her on the ground. She tried to ignore the voice in her head that pointed out just how sexy it was to have a man pick her up like that. "Thank you."

The entranceway was crowded. He took her hand and led her through inside the restaurant. His hand was firm, yet gentle. She could have easily pulled away, but she enjoyed the feel of her hand in his.

They were seated downstairs in the bar area.

"Would you like a drink?" He offered.

"Just water."

"You sure? I don't mind."

She shook her head. "Water's fine."

She ordered four-cheese pasta, and he ordered fettuccini.

"Thanks for getting me out of my apartment." Danielle said, sipping her water. "But I really would have been okay."

"I'm sure you would, but I would never have forgiven myself for letting you spend your birthday by yourself. In my family, it's not allowed."

"That's nice. My mother always did something, but my dad was often flying."

"Pilots do tend to put flying ahead of everything else sometimes. I don't think it's on purpose."

"I don't either."

Danielle caught a clear whiff of grilled meat as a server went by, and the nausea slammed through her again. She put her hand over her mouth.

"Are you okay?"

"I need to get to the restroom."

"It's over there." He pointed, then stood up. "I'll go with you."

He grabbed her handbag off the seat and escorted her to the restroom. She wasn't sure she would have made it without his help leading the way. But she did. And she was sick.

8

*S*amuel stood outside the restroom door and waited for her.

An older woman came out. "Is that your girl in there?"

"Yes."

"There's no one else in there if you want to go in. I can watch the door."

"Thank you." He rushed into the restroom and found her kneeling over a wastebasket. He held her hair. Then, when she was finished, he got her a wet towel.

"Better?"

"Yes. How did you get in here?"

"Someone's watching the door. If you're okay, I'm going to step out."

She nodded as he helped her stand up. "I'm good now."

A few minutes later, she rejoined Samuel in the hallway.

"Do you feel like eating? We don't have to stay."

She looked up at him. "Actually I'm really hungry now."

They sat at the table, and Samuel quietly studied her. That was twice in one day that she'd thrown up. Twice that *he* knew of. He wouldn't be insensitive and ask if there were other times. And now she was fine. Hungry even.

And he had a flashback to his sister's pregnancy. She'd done the exact same thing.

Danielle pregnant?

She smiled at him.

He didn't know her well enough to know. But even if she was, he still wanted to spend time with her. To get to know her.

He was enchanted.

9

*D*anielle was humiliated. But she had enough of her mother in her to hide it behind a smile.

When the food came, she ate half of it, then couldn't eat any more. But that wasn't unusual. It was actually more than she usually ate.

After dinner, they collected his truck from the valet, and he drove them the short distance to the theater.

He watched her closely, and she didn't blame him. She'd only met him today, and already she'd thrown up twice.

He was a perfect gentleman on their non-date date. He bought popcorn and one Coke.

"Maybe this will keep your stomach settled." He handed her the Coke. She sipped and took a small handful of popcorn.

"Do you mind?" He waited for her to shake her head before he took the Coke and sipped. From the straw. The same straw she'd just used.

Now was decision time. She only shared straws with guys she was willing to kiss. When he handed the Coke back, she smiled and put her lips on the straw. She saw him smile out of the corner of her eye.

The movie started shortly. After they put away the soda and popcorn, Danielle tried to focus on the movie. They sat comfortably, like two friends, but Danielle was acutely aware that she was sitting next to him.

She had to keep reminding herself that it wasn't a date. He was just a guy taking pity on her for being alone on her birthday.

Toward the end of the movie, Danielle relaxed and her eyes grew heavy. On top of everything else, it would not be good to fall asleep.

She managed to stay awake, but as the credits rolled on the screen and they stood up, she swayed.

Right into his arms. "Whoa. What happened?" He steadied her back on her feet.

"I don't know. My legs were weak. I was so sleepy."

"You probably wore yourself out being sick all day."

"Probably." Though she didn't feel sick at the moment. Just very, very exhausted. And achy all over.

"I should get you home."

"I think that's a good idea."

Danielle was quiet as they walked out to his truck, and he helped her inside. She gave him directions to her apartment, but otherwise, had little energy for conversation. It was nearly eleven o'clock, and sadly, she admitted to herself that she was usually sound asleep long before this time every night.

He walked her to her door and waited as she unlocked the door and opened it. She stopped, with one foot inside her apartment and one still outside, and turned to him. "Thank you." She smiled into his lovely blue eyes. "Thank you for making this a wonderful birthday."

As she closed the door and locked it behind her, she thought to herself, *I'm not even thinking about kissing him.*

10

There were some things a guy should never ask... or suggest. Growing up with two sisters and a mother in the house, Samuel had picked up a few pointers.

Asking a girl you'd just met if she was pregnant was specifically on that list. Asking a girl who obviously didn't know she was pregnant was not specifically on the list, but he was pretty sure it was contraindicated.

As he stood in line at the corner CVS with a box of Premium saltine crackers in one hand and a bottle of lime-green Gatorade in the other, he wondered how she could possibly not know. He'd heard of girls not knowing they were pregnant, but they were usually girls who were significantly overweight. Danielle was maybe one hundred ten pounds. If she didn't know she was pregnant, it couldn't possibly be long before her clothes started to get a little tight around the waist.

Maybe he should just wait.

In the three days he'd known her, she hadn't done anything that would harm a fetus. She didn't drink alcohol, or smoke cigarettes, or do anything else that would be considered harmful behavior.

Nonetheless, he had two nieces and one nephew, and he had heard more details from his two sisters, who had gone through pregnancies, to know that there were things that needed to be done.

He paid for the crackers and went out to his truck. He was doing everything he could to make sure Danielle ate regular small meals and kept her in crackers to help with the nausea. But she needed to go in for a medical evaluation and she needed to start prenatal vitamins.

He steered his truck out into the traffic to head back to Danielle's office. *I'm not a doctor. Having nieces and nephews does not make me an expert. Leave her alone.*

Feeling good about his decision, he walked across the parking lot and into the building. Besides, it wasn't like she was his girlfriend. She'd said she was never getting back with her ex. *Once a cheater, always a cheater.* But if they were having a baby together, that could very well change things.

Samuel did not want to get in the middle of that. If Jessica had gotten pregnant with their baby and some other guy tried to get involved in it, Samuel would have had to break his jaw. It wouldn't have mattered if they were broken-up or not. The baby would still be theirs – something they made together. What kind of guy would let the mother of his child just walk away?

Samuel's resolve and good intentions lasted another twenty seconds – until he walked into her office and found her sitting on the floor next to the trash can. Her face was pale and her eyes wide as she looked up at him.

"I don't feel so good," she said.

Even if she wasn't pregnant, something was definitely wrong. "I need to get you to the doctor," he said.

She shook her head. "I'll have to call my doctor in Los Angeles, then get my dad to fly me over."

Even to Samuel, a pilot, Danielle's way of thinking baffled

him. It obviously didn't even occur to her to see a doctor in Houston; Houston was home to some of the best doctors in the country.

He smiled to himself. Was this what he had to look forward to with his own child? Did the daughter of a pilot automatically think of flying as the first option for transportation?

He cleared his throat to keep from laughing. Danielle didn't even have a car. She used the city bus system and Uber.

"I can get you in to see a doctor here."

"I don't have a doctor here," she said, as he helped her off the floor and into her chair.

"My sisters go to the Houston Women's Clinic. I can call and get you an appointment."

She didn't say anything. She just watched him with those huge green eyes. *I pushed her too far.* He opened the box of crackers and tore one of the sleeves open. He smiled as he held it out to her. "It's just an offer," he said.

She took a cracker, chewed, and leaned back with her eyes closed. "That might be a lot easier," she said. "I don't really have the energy to make the trip to L.A. right now."

"Do you want me to see if I can get you in tomorrow?" he asked, slipping his cell phone out of his jacket pocket.

"Sure," she said, rubbing her temples. "I didn't know I was going to fall apart at age twenty-three."

He laughed. "I don't think you're falling apart."

She sniffed and sighed. "I think I'm coming down with a cold, too."

Samuel located the phone number of the clinic and dialed. He told himself that his deception was warranted. She doubtlessly thought she would be seeing a primary care physician. He would play dumb when she found out she was seeing an obstetrician.

11

*D*anielle was miserable. She felt like she was coming down with a cold. She was nauseated and throwing up. And she was exhausted. She needed to work on a book cover for Isabella Quinn, but she had zero energy, much less any creativity.

Samuel had dropped her off at her apartment, so now that she was alone, she collapsed on the sofa and, curling her feet beneath her, pulled a throw off the back of the couch and closed her eyes.

She wondered, again, if her father was secretly paying Samuel to watch out for her. He said he was on her father's payroll, but here he was hanging out with her. He couldn't possibly be bored enough to want to spend time with a girl who was always either being sick or complaining about feeling sick.

She would go to his doctor and get something to get past this, then she would be better-able to fight her growing attraction and attachment to this man.

Samuel was nothing like Joey. She'd met Joey when they

were just freshmen in college. That had been ages ago. Her stepfather, Grayson, had inspired Joey to join the military, and she had watched him become a different person. Unlike most guys, the uniform had not been good for Joey. He'd be gone weeks without calling while he was stationed here or there, and they had drifted apart. He'd dropped out of college, and they'd grown even further apart. But then, just when she'd moved on and put him behind her, he'd show up again.

Joey had a certain charm that she wasn't immune to. He would use *we* language and talk about getting married. Danielle considered herself trendy when it came to fashion and hair color. She was the first to jump on the mermaid hair color trend, and she did yoga at least once weekly. She enjoyed her mother's artsy friends. They were so different from Claire, her very traditional mother, that Danielle had been fascinated – like a moth to a flame, she'd studied them and learned about the art world. Not the history of art, but modern art, what attracted people to a painting. Things like that.

She'd switched her major from psychology to fine arts. She had enough of her mother in her to take on a second major, marketing, and so far, the combination was serving her well in the real world of work.

Her downfall had been Joey.

He'd crooked his finger, and she'd followed. *Come join me in Houston. We'll have so much to do. It'll be fun.*

She should've known better. She knew him well enough to know that *come join me* did not translate into *come be with me and be my girl.*

At least not in the sense of any depth. He wanted her to be his girl, alright, for just about three days.

Then he'd recruited a young eighteen-year-old into his bed.

Danielle wasn't shocked. She pretended to be. But she knew he'd been playing around on her ever since he put on that uniform and went off to basic training in San Antonio. A girl could tell those things.

Instead of being shocked, she'd been repulsed.

She wondered now why she suddenly developed repulsion toward her on-and-off boyfriend of five years. Perhaps it was the detail of walking into his apartment and finding him in bed with a young girl, kissing her on the stomach.

Still… not a complete shock.

There were rose petals tossed all over the room. Rose petals? Joey had never used such a romantic gesture with Danielle. Not even once.

When she stripped it down to the bare bones – and Danielle had taken plenty of time to dissect her feelings – it wasn't finding him with the girl. It was finding him with the girl in the very same bed where they had made love the night before.

The. Very. Same. Sheets.

And rose petals?

He'd told Danielle that he loved her. He always did that when they were intimate. He would tell her when he thought she was asleep.

And that was the one detail that tripped her up every time. Because he told her when he thought she was asleep, she believed him.

She believed that even though he wasn't ready to commit, that he still loved her more than anyone else.

She'd thought he would commit eventually.

The old Danielle, back when she was a teenager, hadn't been very good at coping. In high school, while her mother had been out at a gallery event, and her father had been with his new girlfriend, Danielle had been alone after a breakup with a boy she'd particularly liked. His name was Richard, and he'd completely swept her off her feet. She had thought they were going to get married. He was five years older and was a pilot she'd met through her father. She'd had enough sense to never tell her father those two details. Even after weeks of family therapy, she kept those details to herself. In retrospect, she'd sensed it was rather Freudian. She hadn't known about Freud at the time, but she had known that her father didn't need to know.

Nonetheless, in a moment of desperation, she'd taken her mother's Xanax and mixed it with her father's bourbon. That had led to intense individual and family therapy during a mental health hospitalization. It was not a time in her life that she ever wanted to repeat.

She'd lost track of the number of boyfriends she'd been through since then, Joey not included. She suffered through many breakups, but none of them had taxed her coping skills like the one with that pilot. He had been her first sexual experience, and her last, until that night with Joey five weeks ago.

All in all, Danielle's adventurous spirit with clothes, hair, and even in some ways, her career, didn't cross over into her world of relationships.

She dated. A lot. But she rarely crossed that line. With Joey, she'd still been young and vulnerable when their relationship started. She couldn't explain why she'd kept going back to him.

But just because she'd slept with him, didn't mean she couldn't let him go.

Over. With.

She was over Joey.

Somehow the process of being over her long-time on-off boyfriend had led to her needing to take a break from all men.

She hadn't decided how long this self-imposed hiatus was going to last. There was currently no expiration date.

So here she was, vulnerable from her breakup with Joey, when Samuel waltzed in with his innocent sweetness.

Such was the story of her life. Joey had waltzed in when she was vulnerable from her brush with suicide, and Samuel waltzed in after her discontinuation of what she now knew was a toxic relationship with Joey.

Only this time, she was better at coping. If she just didn't have this cold. Or virus. Or whatever it was that was making her sick. She'd felt *off* since that morning nearly six weeks ago. She'd gotten up while Joey was still asleep, gotten dressed, and while it was still dark outside, slipped outside and taken an Uber to her apartment.

As the Uber pulled up to her apartment, she realized her phone was on Joey's bar, so she'd gone straight back to get it.

That's when she'd discovered the whole Joey the scumbag episode.

She'd decided to just calmly get her phone leave.

She hadn't looked back. She had gotten into the Uber that waited for her and gone straight back to her apartment. On the drive back, she'd blocked Joey's number, then on second thought, deleted his number from her phone.

DANIELLE WOKE THE NEXT MORNING ON THE COUCH AND reached for her cell phone on the coffee table. She blinked against the sunlight streaming in through the patio doors. Since she was on the tenth floor of her apartment building, she didn't bother closing the blinds at night. She liked the view of the city lights below.

It was eight o'clock. She'd been asleep for nearly fifteen hours. Samuel would be there to pick her up at eleven. She needed to shower and get herself together. Sitting up, she groaned. It was never a good idea to sleep on the couch. Every muscle ached from sleeping so long on the uncomfortable couch.

Fifteen hours! How was that even possible? She stumbled to the bathroom to take a shower. The hot water on her aching muscles helped. After stepping out of the shower, she tied the towel around her and walked to the kitchen where she had left the package of saltine crackers Samuel had given her.

Her doctor's appointment was at one o'clock. That gave them time for a quick lunch.

Unfortunately, right now, the very thought of food left her feeling ill.

12

*S*amuel knew it was Noah calling before he even looked at his phone. His new boss had a special ring tone.

"I know I promised you this week for moving," Noah said as a greeting. "But can you make a quick run for me?"

Oh no! "Today?"

"Yeah," Noah said.

"I can't."

There was silence on the other end.

Samuel made the quick decision to appeal to Noah's emotional side. "I promised to help Danielle with something."

He heard what sounded like a sigh on the other end of the phone. "Well, can it wait until tomorrow?"

"No. Tomorrow's Saturday. I can fly tomorrow if you need me to."

"It needs to be today," Noah said.

"I'm sorry," Samuel said. "I can't let Danielle down."

"Alright," Noah relented. "I'll see if I can get someone else."

"Great. If I'd known ahead of time…"

"We talked about this Samuel," Noah said. "You have to be available at a moment's notice."

"It's your daughter, Mr. Worthington. It's important."

"She's okay?" He asked, alarm in his voice.

"She's okay," Samuel said. "But I'm picking her up at eleven for an appointment. If I'm not there, she'll have to take the bus."

"Yeah," he said, his voice softening. "She has an aversion to driving."

"She told me she never drives."

"She told you the truth. Her mother and I tried giving her a car years ago. It sat in the garage. I think she took it out once when I insisted she drive me to the airport."

Samuel laughed. "Maybe she prefers flying."

"Maybe." Noah hesitated. "Take care of my girl. I'll find someone else for the flight."

Samuel hung up and sighed with relief. He hadn't said anything that wasn't true. He'd merely sketched around the truth. It was the right thing to do anyway. It wasn't his place to disclose Danielle's business. But if Noah sent him off flying today, Danielle wouldn't make her doctor's appointment, and his gut told him she'd put off going altogether.

Glancing at the time, he showered, shaved, and put on a pair of jeans and a polo shirt. It may be November, but it was warm today in typical Houston weather.

He reminded himself, on the drive over to pick up Danielle, that he was doing this for Noah. His employer's daughter needed help, and since he was on the payroll, he was honor-bound to take care of her.

When he pulled up to the door of her apartment building, Danielle was standing outside waiting for him.

She was wearing a flowing lavender dress splashed with a bouquet of flowers and a little matching sweater. She looked incredibly feminine. His heart stuttered just a little as she smiled at him.

He pulled up and got out of the truck, meeting her on the passenger side. She was wearing flats today, so the top of her head barely reached his shoulders. He opened the door and helped her climb inside. When she put her hand on his arm before stepping into the truck, she looked up at him and smiled.

The flash of attraction was unmistakable. He not only wanted to take care of her, he wanted to know what it felt like to kiss her.

These were feelings he'd thought he'd buried with Jessica.

His boss's daughter was not the one for him to be having these thoughts and feelings about. If they were going to resurface, they needed to resurface with someone else.

Once she was inside the truck, he closed the door and pulled himself together as he walked around to the driver's side.

"Where would you like to eat lunch?" he asked.

She grinned sheepishly. "Pappa's Burgers?"

If he'd learned one thing, it was to never question a woman's food cravings – pregnant or not. "Alright," he said. "Pappa's it is."

He saw her expression of relief out of the corner of his eye.

As they waited for their shrimp po'boys to arrive, Samuel said, "You look like you're feeling better."

"I am," she agreed. "The crackers help."

He smiled. "I'll tell my mother. She'll be happy to know that her insistence that I keep crackers in my truck paid off."

Danielle chuckled.

"Did you find out what happened to that model you were expecting?"

"No," she said. "Sometimes they get cold feet." She shrugged. "Really? That's odd."

"It's kind of an odd business."

"Do you work for yourself?"

"Sort of, but not really. Sort of like you and my father, actually."

"How so?"

"I work for a company called 'Show Don't Tell Book Covers.' They do all the advertising and handle the office. I make my covers and submit them to the office manager, who posts them on a website. I make a percentage."

"Why not just do it yourself?" Samuel sipped his soda.

"Because I'm new at it. A lot of designers spin off their own companies."

"So once you get established, that's something you might think about doing?"

"Maybe. What about you? Are you thinking about starting your own company?"

He waited while the server dropped their food off. Then dipped a French fry into ketchup before tasting it. "I don't know. I'm not sure I want the overhead." He met her gaze. "As you may be aware, airplanes are rather costly."

She chuckled. "I suppose there is quite a difference between buying an airplane and buying a computer. I'd still have to hire models though, just like he hires pilots."

"I guess we have similar business models." He took a bite of his sandwich. It was good, but he truly hoped she got around to wanting to try something new for lunch, sooner rather than later.

Then he caught himself. It had been so easy to just slip into a routine with Danielle. They'd meet for lunch, then work around her office until she was ready to go home, then he'd drive her to her apartment building and drop her off. She hadn't invited him up, so their activities had been restricted to lunch and afternoons.

It was for the best.

She was the boss's daughter.

Samuel was smart enough to know better.

But her being the boss's daughter was a double-edged sword. He needed to keep his distance, but he also needed to watch out for her.

He had a feeling Noah had no idea how much Danielle needed watching after. She ate half her sandwich, just like yesterday. He picked up the other half and finished it off. He only shrugged when she smirked at him.

"You know, I was thinking." She smiled at the waiter when he stopped at their table.

"Can I get you a hand-made milkshake?" The waiter asked hopefully.

Her eyes lit up. "Hmm. That sounds good. What do you think, Samuel?"

"Sure," he agreed, pushing his empty plate aside. It was a good thing he had a high metabolism.

She ordered a chocolate milkshake, and he ordered vanilla.

"You said you were thinking about something?" Though he'd thought it was a little unusual at the time, he now found the little swirl of lavender highlights in her hair quite charming.

He liked the way her eyes lit up when she had a new idea.

"I feel better today. I haven't thrown up at all. Maybe I don't need to go to the doctor."

"Oh no." This was not one of her *good* new ideas. "The way you've been sick all week, you should get checked out. Just to make sure."

She wrinkled her nose. Then sighed. "All right. But only because you're going in with me."

Samuel coughed as the Coke he was swallowing went down the wrong way. Oh no! This was not going to backfire on him like this.

There was no way he was going to go in with her to see the gynecologist.

"Are you okay?" She reached out and touched his hand as regained his composure.

He held up his hand. "I'm good."

The waiter brought their milkshakes.

She sipped. Wrinkled her nose again. "I think this one is yours." She pushed her glass to him and traded.

Samuel picked up the glass and stared at the straw a moment. Her lips had just been on this straw. He had a rule. Never drink after anyone unless he was willing to kiss them. Sucking on this straw was going to be almost like kissing her. They'd shared a soda during the movie, and that had led to him thinking about kissing he even more.

Without thinking about it any further, he took a deep sip of the milkshake.

"Do you like it?" She asked.

He closed his eyes and let his breath out slowly. When he opened his eyes and looked into hers, he knew he was in more trouble than he'd thought.

13

*A*s Danielle sipped her milkshake, she studied Samuel over the top of her glass. He had suddenly started squirming.

"Are you okay?" She watched his eyes dart to hers, then to the traffic outside the window.

"Yeah." He looked back at her. "I'm good."

"I'm glad you're going in with me," she said.

He scrubbed a hand across his chin. "I'm not sure that's a good idea."

"Why not?" She was curious now. What was making this guy uncomfortable? Ever since she mentioned him going in with her, he'd avoided eye contact.

"That might not be a good idea."

"Why not?" She asked.

"I don't know you all that well."

She scoffed. "We've had lunch together almost every day this week. I think we know each other well enough. I mean..." She set her glass down and realized with a measure of embarrassment that she'd already drank half of it. "'Besides...

I've thrown up in front of you. I don't think it gets much more intimate than that."

He coughed again. Then managed to look into her eyes again. "I think it can get much more intimate."

Now it was her turn to squirm. Well… when he put it like that…

"It's not like I have to get undressed or anything."

He was studying the traffic again. Sipping his milkshake. "You never know," he muttered against his straw.

He glanced at his phone. "Speaking of appointments, I think we better get going."

"We haven't finished our milkshakes," she pointed out.

"We'll get them to go." He motioned for the server and within minutes, they had fresh milkshakes in paper cups.

"I don't know what's wrong with me," she said against her straw. "I don't normally eat desserts."

"We'll see what the doctor says," he said, ushering her toward the front door.

"I have to make a quick stop," she said before she darted into the restroom.

Staring at her reflection as she washed her hands, she wondered what a mess he must think of her. She threw up all the time. She ate like a bird one minute, then a starving person the next, and she went to the bathroom all the time.

A thought darted at the edge of her consciousness, but she pushed it away. A virus. That's all it was.

14

_____

The minute she walked through the door, Danielle knew the Houston Women's Clinic was not a doctor's office for colds and viruses. It was a female clinic in every sense of the word.

Samuel hadn't said much on the drive over. *He knew.* He knew he was bringing her to a gynecologist. Surely, he didn't think she was seeing a primary care doctor here? If he did, he was desperately misinformed.

"Have you been here before?" She stepped into the elevator and waited while he pressed the button. With his lack of hesitation in guiding them to the fourth floor, she already knew the answer to her question.

"Yes." He glanced at her, then stared at the elevator door. "My younger sister got divorced shortly after becoming pregnant, so I came with her to all her appointments.

"Ah-ha!"

He turned and looked at her quizzically. "Ah-ha what?"

Danielle got in line to check in. "You knew," she hissed. She took the clipboard from the clerk, and he followed her to a secluded area of the waiting room.

"I knew what?" He nudged her elbow when she quietly began writing in her name.

She looked up beneath her lashes. His gaze locked onto hers now. She squinted, unsure how she felt about the fact that he had brought her to a gynecologist when she'd thought he'd made an appointment for her with a family doctor.

"Samuel." She stood the clipboard on her knees. Nodded toward the waiting room. There were no one but females, and two of them were clearly pregnant. She leaned toward him. Whispered. "Do you think I'm pregnant?"

He ran his hands along his thighs, keeping his eyes straight ahead. "I don't know."

She lowered her head and focused on the paperwork, letting her hair cascade around her face. She bit her lip as she filled in her address and date of birth.

He turned back to her. "Is it possible?"

She bit her lip and focused on family history. Nothing to report. All were healthy.

Is it possible?

That was the question that had been darting around her mind all morning.

She had to admit that, yes, it was possible.

The other question was whether it was likely.

She turned the page and signed her name at the bottom of the form.

Without looking at Samuel, she stood up and took the clipboard to the reception desk. Then she turned and went back to sit next to Samuel and began digging in her handbag for her lip gloss.

She felt him staring at her. Waiting.

Waiting for her to reveal whether or not she'd been sexually active. And pregnant. If not pregnant, she had some kind of terrible disease. Even as she sat there, avoiding answering Samuel's pointed question, she felt sick. Again.

She heaved a sigh. And turned to face him.

At least he was looking at her again. "I don't know," she shrugged.

He scowled. "How can you not know?" He sat back, a knowing expression forming on his face. "If you don't know, that means it's possible."

"I don't know can mean a lot of things," Danielle said as her phone chimed, indicating a Facebook message. It was from Isabella Quinn, her author client who was waiting for a cover. Her only author client at the moment.

She read the message and rolled her eyes. "That's never going to happen."

"What?"

"The author wants the couple on her cover to be kissing."

Samuel laughed. "So? It's a romance cover."

"Jacob and Avery can't stand the sight of each other, much less to kiss."

"You said they worked well together, they'll just see it as a normal part of their job. Like any actor."

"You're right," she said, messaging Isabella back. *We have another shoot tomorrow. I'll make it happen.*

"Danielle Worthington." A nurse called her name.

Danielle stood up and held out her hand to Samuel. "Come on," she insisted.

He didn't move.

"It's okay," the nurse said. "We welcome husbands."

"I'm not…" Samuel began, but blew out his breath and took her hand.

Danielle smiled at the nurse as she went through the door and followed the nurse to the exam room.

15

———

*S*amuel had been here before.

But it was not a place he wanted to be with Danielle.

His mother would call it *improper*. Danielle was about to take off her clothes and be examined.

For pregnancy.

And he'd only known her for four days. She was his boss's daughter.

There were so many things wrong with this scenario, his flittering brain cells didn't know which wrong to light upon.

He forced himself to listen as Danielle described her symptoms to the nurse. He'd brought her here after all. It was the least he could do.

She turned and smiled sweetly at him. "Did I miss anything?"

He shook his head and wondered if he looked as uncomfortable as he felt.

"Everything off," the nurse said, slid the curtain closed, and stepped from the room. The curtain that separated Samuel from Danielle.

"Do you want me to step out?" *Please say yes.*

"Don't you dare leave me," Danielle said from the other side of the curtain.

He heard rustling as she began to undress. How long would it be before they had the results of the pregnancy test? She would have to do blood work. A couple of days?

She hadn't answered his question. The paradox was, that by saying she didn't know if she was pregnant, this told him that she could be.

There were many implications involved in this situation.

"Are you still here?" Danielle called as he heard her step onto the exam table.

"I'm right here," he answered. The thought of her sitting on the other side of the curtain wearing nothing more than a paper dress nearly sent him into a tailspin.

I shouldn't be thinking about her that way. She's Noah's daughter. My boss's daughter.

"Samuel?"

He knew that tone. She was going to be sick. *I shouldn't know this.*

"I'm going to be sick."

The words spurred him into action. He looked around for a trash can, but didn't see one. He only had seconds. Walking backwards, he went to the other side of the curtain.

And found the trash can. He slid it next to her and used his foot to open the lid.

He had made it in time.

He held her hair while keeping his gaze on the wall. Out of habit, he put a hand on her back and nearly jerked back as his fingers touched bare skin. So soft.

The doctor came in just at that moment.

"Oh my," she said.

Grateful to have the distraction, Samuel looked at Dr. Neal. He recognized her from bringing in his sister. She was young, probably mid-thirties, and always had a smile on her face.

The doctor moistened a towel with water and handed it to Danielle to wipe her face. "Has this been happening a lot?" she asked.

"A little," Danielle said.

"All the time," Samuel said.

He looked at her then, wearing her paper gown, her hair flowing around her, one hand holding the wet paper towel. His heart tripped over itself. He took the towel from her and gently wiped her mouth.

"Thank you," she whispered, when he finished.

"Let's take a look," Dr. Neal said.

Samuel ducked back behind the curtain and pulled out his phone. Their voices were muted, and he checked his email to distract himself from listening in to what they were saying.

"How's your sister?" Dr. Neal asked, as she stepped out from behind the curtain.

"She's great," Samuel said, more than a little surprised that Dr. Neal remembered him.

"Take good care of this one."

"I will," Samuel said. "Thank you."

"Only a couple more days before you know if you're going to be a daddy."

---

16

*D*anielle pulled her shirt over her head. The door closed, and they were alone again.

"Are you okay?" Samuel asked from the other side of the curtain.

"Yeah," she said. "I'll just be a minute." She hadn't realized just how nervous she'd been. Even after the examination, she really didn't know anything more than she had when she came in.

She could hear him pacing while she slipped into her sneakers and tied the shoelaces. "What now?" he asked.

"Bloodwork."

"Right."

Fully dressed, she stepped from behind the curtain. He stopped pacing and faced her. His hair was all over the place and his shirt was... crooked. She laughed. "You look like a mess."

"Thanks." He straightened his shirt. "You look... beautiful."

She bit her lip and tried to ignore the little thrill that shot through her at his unexpected words. "I guess I don't have a virus."

"Did she say anything?"

Danielle shrugged. "She'll call with the bloodwork results."

"Good. Hey. Why did she say that?" He opened the door and held it while she walked through.

"Why she said what?"

He shook his head. "Never mind."

Danielle hadn't corrected Dr. Neal's assumption that Samuel was the father of her possible baby.

She took the prescription for prenatal vitamins and shoved it into her handbag. She hadn't answered Samuel's question, but, yes, it was possible that she was pregnant.

The fact that she and Joey had been intimate the very night before she walked in on him with that girl was like running sandpaper over a paper cut. It hurt like hell, and she didn't want to even think about it.

They got on the elevator and went downstairs to the packed lab area.

If she was pregnant with Joey's child, he would never know it. She wanted nothing to do with him. And she was pretty sure he would want nothing to do with the child… or with her.

"Danielle?" Samuel touched her arm. "They called your name."

She stood up, but instead of going to the lab door, she waited for him. When he didn't stand up, she tugged on his elbow.

He chuckled and followed her to where the nurse waited. "I don't think I'm supposed to go back there," he said.

The nurse shook her head. "They try to get out of it all the time."

"It's good to know it's not just me."

She sat in the chair, pulled up her sleeve, held her other hand out to Samuel, who stood next to her. She scrunched up her face. "Ouch!"

The nurse chuckled. "I haven't even started."

"I know," Danielle said. "But I don't like needles."

"Not many do."

As the nurse stuck the needle in her arm, she clenched Samuel's hand.

"This is going to be fun. If, you know…" he said.

She glanced down at her arm to the blood flowing through the tube. He followed her gaze.

Then Samuel passed out on the floor.

17

*S*amuel was fairly certain he would never live it down.

He pulled the blanket over his head and decided it was a good day to sleep in. It was Saturday, and he had nothing to do. No plans. Not even with Danielle.

Danielle.

She was working today.

He groaned.

How was she going to get to the photo shoot location?

She would ride the bus. Like she always did.

Or use Uber.

He hated the thought of her riding the bus or even using Uber. It was supposed to be safe, but still…

He threw off the blanket and made his way to the shower. He stood under the hot water until it began to cool.

Who was he kidding? He wasn't about to stay away from her today. He smiled to himself. Not even the embarrassment of literally passing out at the sight of blood could keep him from wanting to see her.

She hadn't laughed at him. She'd done nothing but show

concern. Nonetheless, it had been embarrassing to wake up on the floor after passing out.

That wasn't exactly the image he wanted to portray. He heated a cup of coffee and sent her a text. *Need a ride to the park?*

Two minutes later, his phone chimed with a response. *Already there.*

Did you take your car? He added a smiley face emoticon.

Ha. Yes. The one in L.A.?

He ran a hand through his still-damp hair. She was exasperating. Probably a lot like her father. He hadn't considered it until now, but with the exception of yesterday when he'd taken her to the doctor, most of their time together had been spent doing her work.

Samuel hadn't known very many women quite so driven to achieve.

Impressive.

He popped two pieces of bread in the toaster while he tied his boots. He couldn't very well leave her stranded out there. Not when he had a perfectly good truck.

As he maneuvered through the Saturday morning traffic, it occurred to him that he hadn't set foot in an airplane in over a week. He hadn't gone that long without being off the ground since... well... ever. At least not since he'd gotten his pilot's license.

And he'd barely even thought about it.

In fact, he'd thought about little other than Danielle since he'd met her.

He parked his car and walked to the little white house where he knew she'd be. It was a perfect day to be outside. The temperature had just enough of a nip that he was glad he wore his blue jean jacket. Red and gold leaves from an oak tree skittered about his feet. Fall was hands-down his favorite time of year. The new school year brought new beginnings. Anything was possible.

He knew something was wrong before he could even hear what they were saying.

The male model, Samuel couldn't remember his name, was pacing.

Samuel was pretty sure pacing didn't make the best photos.

When he was in earshot, he stopped, and, stepping off the path, stood next to a tree, watching the interaction.

The male model paced back and faced Danielle. Samuel's nerves went on alert. It had been awhile since he'd been in a physical scuffle. Not that he made a habit of fighting. Only twice, to be exact, and both in college, but he wasn't opposed to tackling anyone who threatened someone he cared about.

Cared about. He'd have to think about that later. Danielle had her hair pulled back today and she wore a bright blue pea coat. Her skin glowed with the crisp fall air.

"I won't do it," Jacob said.

Danielle stood her ground, one hand on her hip and the other holding her camera. "Okay," she said. "Just pretend."

Jacob shook his head, turned away. Samuel relaxed a little.

Avery, who stood a few feet from Danielle, glared at Jacob. "He won't do it," she said.

"It's just a job," Danielle said. "It's not like you have to like each other."

Jacob turned back and glared at both women. "You know what," he said. "I don't even need this job. I don't have to be here, and I don't have to do this. I quit." He turned on his heel and walked away.

The girls watched as he strode down the path that led to the park's exit. Samuel got back on the path and approached them. "Hey," he said. "What's going on?"

Danielle turned, and he saw the frustration on her face. "Jacob just quit."

"Why?" Why would he walk off a job where all he had to do

was stand around and be photographed with one pretty girl by another gorgeous female?

"He didn't want to kiss me." Avery rolled her eyes.

"Right," he said. Danielle had mentioned something about the author she was working with needing a kissing scene. He'd forgotten about that. Danielle's doctor's visit had distracted him from thinking about anything else. "Just find someone else, right?"

Both women stared at him.

"Surely it can't be that hard to find someone who'll kiss Avery."

They looked at each other and after a beat, they both burst out laughing.

"It can't be just anyone," Avery pointed out.

"The author is going to flip," Danielle said. "She loved the chemistry between Avery and Jacob."

"If she only knew," Avery muttered.

"Now we have to start over with a new model."

18

*D*anielle studied Samuel. He hadn't shaved today. He had just enough shadow to give him that certain bad-boy look that she found irresistible. The same thought occurred to her that she'd had when she first saw him. *He would look good on a book cover.*

Women would definitely drool over him. Not that she was drooling. Well, maybe just a little.

Maybe she could talk him into posing – just for this author. Not that he would want to be a model. She knew enough about pilots to know that they were single-minded. In fact, she wondered why he was here and not off flying somewhere.

He caught her looking at him, and his eyes widened. He shook his head just enough for her to know that he knew what she was thinking.

"Samuel," she smiled sweetly. "Let me take a few pictures of you and Avery and send them to the author."

Now he was shaking his head in earnest. "I'm not a model."

"You don't have to be a model. You just have to let me photograph you."

"To be on a book cover," he glanced at Avery. "with her."

"Seriously," Avery crossed her arms. "Do I have a wart on my nose or something today?"

Danielle tore her gaze away from Samuel long enough to respond. "You're beautiful Avery. He's just being difficult. And Jacob… well… you would know better than I what's going on with him."

Avery rolled her eyes. "Yeah. You don't want to know."

"It's hard working with someone you have a history with." Danielle shrugged.

Avery had a stunned look on her face. As if everyone couldn't see it. Danielle turned back to Samuel. "Maybe I could take a couple and text them. If she says no, it's a moot point."

Samuel glanced at Avery and seemed to consider. Danielle swallowed a flash of regret. Samuel with Avery together in a photograph, much less on a book cover for all of eternity. Maybe this wasn't such a good idea after all.

She was about to open her mouth and say they would look for other options when Samuel said. "Okay."

"Okay? You'll do it?" Her emotions were all over the place. In that moment, she truly hoped she was pregnant, so she could blame it on that. She didn't want to admit that although it would help her out professionally if he said yes, she had truly hoped he wouldn't do it.

Avery was gorgeous, and Samuel was handsome. They were going to make a great couple. How could the author not want them on her book cover? Together.

She nodded and let professionalism win. "Go stand next to each other on the porch."

Lifting her camera, she watched them through the lens. Avery was looking at Samuel, but Samuel was watching her, not Avery.

"You have to look at Avery," she said.

Samuel turned his gaze toward Avery. *Good.* She took

several pictures. Zoomed in. They did look good together. Avery reached out and put an arm on Samuel's.

Danielle was going to be sick. Right now. She lowered the camera and turned around.

By the time she was hurling the contents of her breakfast, Samuel was there, holding her hair. "Thank you," she murmured.

Danielle sat on the porch steps. *If I'm not pregnant, I have something terribly wrong with me.*

"Are you okay?" Avery asked. This was the first time Danielle had been sick around her.

"I think I must have a virus," Danielle took a tissue from her handbag and wiped her mouth.

"I'll get you some water," Samuel darted away.

"I hope I don't catch it," Avery said.

Danielle didn't answer. She didn't tell Avery that she wasn't contagious.

Within minutes, Samuel was back with water… and crackers.

"Let's take a break, Avery. Come back at one o'clock. By then I should have an answer from the author." Danielle pulled up the pictures, picked out three, and sent them to the author.

"No problem," Avery said, gathering up her backpack and heading down the path to her car.

Danielle nibbled a cracker and sipped from the bottle of water.

"Better?" Samuel brought over her tripod.

She nodded. "Thank you."

He sat down beside her. He rubbed her back, right between her shoulder blades. *No. I will not be attracted to Samuel. I can like him, but I'm not attracted to anyone right now.*

A dating moratorium. She might even be pregnant. Not a good time to be crushing on her father's new employee. A pilot at that. A pilot that was helping her out by posing as a model with her best girl model.

The nausea had passed, but she was still feeling unsettled. Seeing them gazing at each other had been too much. Had it been the possible pregnancy or just seeing them together? She really needed to get that question answered. Maybe she would get an over-the-counter pregnancy test on the way home and take that. She needed to know what was going on with her. Just so she knew how to interpret all these emotions going on with her.

When she was around Samuel.

Suddenly, a little golden retriever puppy was racing toward her. The puppy jumped into her lap and began licking her face. Danielle laughed.

A little girl, about five, was running toward her with her mother right behind her.

"Rex!" The little girl ran up to Danielle.

The puppy jumped out of Danielle's arms to nip around the little girl's heels. She squealed in delight.

The woman, winded, caught up with them. She smiled at Danielle. "Thank you so much."

"You're welcome, but I didn't do anything."

"My daughter loves this puppy." She held up the harness. "I don't know how he managed to get loose."

"He's adorable."

The woman knelt and wrangled the dog back into his harness. "Do you two have children?" Her daughter danced around them.

Danielle glanced at Samuel and shook her head.

"Well, don't wait too long. The older you get, the harder it is to keep up with them."

"I would imagine It's hard at any age."

The woman held her daughter's hand with one hand and

the puppy's leash with the other. "Again, thank you for helping."

"Bye!" The little girl grinned and waved as she walked away.

"Cute." Danielle said. "Do you have any pets?"

"My mom has a couple of cats, but no, I don't. Do you?"

"I have a cat at my mom's. His name is Charlie. I miss him terribly."

"Maybe your mom can bring him for a visit."

"Maybe." Danielle stared after the girl with the dog.

Samuel glanced at his watch. "Want to get some lunch?"

"Sounds good." Anything to distract her from the direction of her thoughts.

They walked together down the path to his truck. "Do you mind stopping by the drug store when you take me home?"

"Of course not."

Her phone beeped. "She's already responded."

"That was fast."

"Yeah, unusual." Danielle slid open her messages. Looked up at Samuel. "She loves it."

"You don't seem happy about it."

Danielle shrugged. "I've put a lot of work into the images with Avery and Jacob. I even had a mock up done. I didn't know she was gonna want them kissing."

"Why wouldn't Jacob kiss Avery?"

"I don't know details, but they have a history."

"Still… if he's kissed her before…"

"I guess kissing is intimate for some people."

He gave her a lopsided grin. "I thought kissing was intimate for everyone."

Her face flushed. "Maybe he didn't want to risk opening up old feelings. Or maybe he just really doesn't like her."

"Guess we'll never know."

She took a deep breath. "So now you get to kiss Avery."

He stopped walking. She took two steps and turned back.

He looked a little stunned. "What? You didn't put this together?"

"I guess I hadn't thought it through. It was kind of sudden."

Danielle took it as a good sign that he hadn't been looking forward to kissing Avery. In fact, she liked it that he didn't look any too happy about the whole situation.

By the time they reached his truck, she had a little bounce back in her step.

19

*S*amuel did not want to kiss Avery. First of all, she was too young. Second, she was blonde. And third, he didn't know her.

And fourth, she wasn't Danielle.

He surely didn't want to kiss her in front of Danielle. Something about that felt distinctly off.

He hadn't kissed anyone since Jessica. So that meant it had been years since he'd kissed anyone.

The whole train of thought just about sent him into a tailspin.

Since they were on the other side of town, and neither of them were familiar with the area, they found a little Mexican restaurant. Being the first ones there, they picked a booth in the back.

Danielle leaned back and put her feet on his bench. Who was going to rub her feet? From being around his sisters, he knew that pregnant women needed their feet rubbed. Often.

Danielle was going to be a single mom. And she was an only child. He didn't know a lot about the rest of her social life.

"When you moved from L.A., did you leave behind any friends?"

She shook her head. "Between work and my family and boyfriend, I didn't have any time left over. Besides," she shrugged. "I've never really been the type to go out with girlfriends."

She was similar to Jessica in that way. Jessica hadn't had girlfriends either. With her being in the military especially, all her friends were male, but she didn't go out either. Unless she was with him.

So far, that was the only similarity he'd discovered between the two girls. Danielle wore makeup and painted her nails. Her hair was highlighted in a trendy fashion. Jessica never wore makeup and never even went to a nail salon that he knew of. She kept her short hair pulled back most of the time.

"What about you?" She asked. "You have a guy friend that you hang out with?"

"Nah. My family keeps me occupied when I'm not flying."

"Speaking of. Aren't you supposed to be packing and getting ready to move to Dallas?"

"I'm packed," he said, "but don't tell your dad. He gave me two weeks, and I'm going to stay here as long as I possibly can."

"There really weren't any jobs in Houston?"

"There was a teaching job open, but I can't see myself teaching others to fly. I'd miss being in the air by myself."

"You sound a lot like my dad. He's only happy when he's flying. Or with his new wife Savannah." She wrinkled her nose.

"You don't like her?"

"Oh yeah. She's great, and my dad has been in love with her since the day they met at college. But it's just weird thinking about him being with someone."

"I'm lucky, I guess. My parents have stayed together. As far as I know, they're happy together."

"You are lucky. My parents didn't like each other very

much. Their marriage was a business arrangement." He made a face. "I didn't know this until after they got divorced. I just knew that my father was rarely home, and when he was home, I did things with him. We rarely did things as a family. It was almost like they were divorced, but living in the same house."

"Yuck."

"It was life as I knew it. I didn't know it was supposed to be any different."

"Your ex, what's his name?"

"Joey." She scowled. "But ex is a good name for him."

"Are you going to tell him about the baby?"

"If there's a baby," she corrected. "No. Absolutely not."

"I'd want to know," he whispered.

"But you're different. You're more settled."

"Are you saying I'm boring?" He scooped a chip into the salsa and tasted it.

"Of course not."

"It's okay. I know I am."

"It's better to be boring than to be a cad." Her face flushed.

There was still some heat there. She pretended to be over this… Joey… but there was some unfinished business. How was she going to cope with having her ex's baby? A man whose name she couldn't even stand to speak.

Joey would find out about the baby. He supposed it was possible that if they never saw each other again, he might not know, but it would be better for Danielle if she chose how he found out. She needed to pick the time and place, and Samuel needed to be with her.

He'd read somewhere that the number one cause of death for pregnant women was murder. Men like Joey, who most likely didn't want a child, could be unpredictable.

He would bring this up after she heard from the doctor.

Right now, he had to figure out what to do about this predicament involving kissing Avery.

20

"*I* changed my mind."

Danielle folded her arms and glared at Avery. "What? What's that supposed to mean?"

"It means no. I'm not kissing…" She gestured toward Samuel. "him."

"What's wrong with him?" Danielle studied Samuel, looking for something she'd missed. Other than his squirming at the moment, she saw absolutely nothing she didn't like.

Avery shrugged.

Danielle put a palm against her forehead and closed her eyes. This was a train wreck that she never saw coming when she got up this morning. It was a beautiful fall day. Perfect for photographing. "What am I supposed to do?" She asked, mostly to herself.

"You kiss him."

Danielle opened her eyes. She looked first at Avery, who wore a smug expression, then at Samuel, who had his eyebrows scrunched together. Her gaze went to his lips. And it was as though Avery's words had breathed life into the most wonderful idea. "Okay," she said and hoped her voice didn't sound as breathy as it felt. She cleared her throat and pulled her gaze from Samuel's lips.

She glanced down. She had on tights and a short skirt. Her jacket was short with a longer shirt layered beneath. Not so very different from what Avery wore. She could work with this.

"You'll have to take the pictures," she handed her camera to Avery. She'd have to do some serious Photoshopping, but this was doable.

The author liked Samuel, so maybe she wouldn't notice that the female model had changed. She'd just put the kissing couple – them – on the cover and send it to her.

Avery went into photographer role. "Let's do some warm-up shots first."

Danielle chuckled as Avery mimicked her.

Samuel wore a baffled expression. "So now *we're* the cover models?"

"Sure. Why not?"

"Why not?" He took her hand and led her halfway up the stairs of the white house. They waited while another couple walked around behind them.

"So we just look at each other?" he asked.

"That's a good start."

"I can do that."

"Try to look happy," she said and took her own advice, putting a smile on her face. Her mother had passed along many of the skills she'd learned in finishing school. Danielle knew how to look happy even in the most uncomfortable of situations.

As she gazed into Samuel's blue eyes, she heard the click of the camera, then she got lost in his eyes, and the rest of the world faded away. Her heart rate went into overdrive.

He took her hand and pulled her closer. Then he put his arms loosely around her. She put her hands on his chest and leaned her elbows against him. Her head tilted up. He was a full head taller than she was. A perfect height. He smelled good, like deep, rich masculinity.

They were close enough that she could feel his breath against her forehead. Her lips parted as he moved toward her. He kissed her forehead.

She swayed toward him. He pulled her closer, and her arms went around his neck. He kissed her cheek. The corner of her mouth.

Danielle thought she heard Avery moving around with the camera, but she didn't care if she took any pictures or not. Right now all she wanted was to feel his lips against hers.

He ran a finger along her bottom lip. Danielle shivered.

Then his lips were pressed against hers.

And she felt the spark all through her body.

He kissed her top lip. Then her bottom lip. Then the edge of her mouth again.

She wanted more. But he pulled away, leaving her feeling bereft.

Then he whispered in her ear. "We can do this later when no one's watching."

She opened her eyes and smiled. That was a lovely idea. More. Later.

Avery continued to snap photos while they smiled at each other.

"Okay, that's a wrap," Avery held the camera out toward Danielle. Danielle tore her gaze away from Samuel and took the camera.

"You two need to get a room," Avery said and bounced down the steps. "Call me if you need me Danielle," she said over her shoulder.

Danielle was blushing. She felt it all the way to her hairline.

"Do you think we made some good photos?" he asked.

"I'll have to look at them." How could he go from that kiss

to having coherent thoughts? Her brain was fried. Just one kiss. Perhaps a moratorium wasn't such a good idea. She was like a person dying of thirst.

He took her hand and led her down the path to his truck. After he helped her inside, he smiled at her, and her heart did a somersault.

She was in serious trouble.

21

They were mostly silent on the drive back to Danielle's apartment. She asked him to wait while she ran into the pharmacy.

That kiss had knocked his socks off. He wanted to see the photos, but he didn't want to seem weird about it. He would ask to see them later.

Right now, he had to figure out how to proceed. Now that he'd kissed her, kissing her again was all he could think about.

Would it be presumptuous to think that he could kiss her again? They'd kissed for a photo. He'd never done that before. He didn't know the protocol.

Was he to pretend like it hadn't happened? Protocol or not, that was never going to happen. Maybe he should wait and give her time to think about it; or not give her time to think about it.

His thoughts circled around until she came back with a small bag, and he decided to follow her lead.

He always walked her to the door, so he did that.

"I need to get to work on this cover." She gripped the bag in one hand as she unlocked the door with the other.

"Sure. Let me know how it turns out."

She smiled over her shoulder. "I will. Thanks for the ride today."

Then she was inside her apartment with the door between them.

He huffed out a sigh.

How could she go from that kiss to just walking away?

22

*D*anielle locked the door and leaned against it. She took deep breaths like her counselor had taught her until her heart rate was back to normal.

She hadn't trusted herself around Samuel. One kiss and all rational thought had left her brain. She needed to get away from him before she threw herself at him.

She really did need to work on the cover. She was hoping the author either wouldn't notice or wouldn't care that Avery was missing from the image. She could take some more with Samuel later if need be.

But right now, she wanted to take the pregnancy test.

She went into her bedroom and curled up on the bed. She read the directions all the way through, then set the test aside. According to the directions, she would have to wait until morning. Apparently, pregnancy tests were more accurate when taken first thing in the morning. It was so tempting to ignore that little detail, but she put it aside and went into her home office and uploaded the pictures from today's shoot. She needed to do the serious work at her larger office computer, but she could at least start looking at the photos, in case they needed to do another shoot.

Avery may not be a photographer, but the photos that she took weren't half bad. She'd captured some really good images.

As Danielle scrolled through the photos, her heart rate increased again. She wanted to devour Samuel, and that was evident in the images.

It was surprising though that he obviously wanted to devour her, too. That kind of desire couldn't be faked. Especially not by someone who had absolutely no training in modeling or acting.

There was one particular image that jumped off the screen. His lips were pressed against her top lip and his hand pressed against her jaw. She hadn't even realized he'd touched her face. That was the image she was going to use.

She saved it to her screen and sat back. They looked good together. Really good.

And they had a connection. Or at least she had felt a connection.

To be fair, she hadn't given him a chance one way or the other. Then she remembered the words he'd whispered in her ear. *We can do this later when no one's watching.*

She scrolled back through their photos. She definitely wanted to do more of that sooner than later. Surely her moratorium had been going on long enough. Maybe it was time to come out of it.

She jumped when her phone rang, and her mother's picture popped up on the screen.

"Hi honey." Her mother sounded quite chipper. Not a good sign. "I'm coming into town next week. Can you have the guest room ready?"

23

*P*appa's Burgers for family dinner. Of all the places in Houston they could have picked for this week's gathering, they picked Pappa's Burgers.

Samuel parked his truck in the crowded parking lot and found his family gathered in the private room. Everyone was there. His older sister and her husband, his younger sister, his brother and his wife, and both sets of grandparents. Both of his sisters had brought their toddlers, too, rounding out four generations. His younger sister had brought a date, so that left Samuel as the only single person there.

Since he was the last one to arrive, he took the only seat left, right between his grandparents. The conversation went along as usual until their food arrived.

That's when the eldest of his two grandmothers, Veronica Johnson, leaned over and whispered near his ear. "When are you going to start bringing a lady friend with you again? We all miss Jessica, but it's been two years."

At least she had the decorum to not broadcast her comment to the whole table. The topic of his dating was one topic he did not want to get his sisters started on. "I'll look into that," he whispered back. "Maybe next time."

Veronica's face brightened. "I hope so. It saddens me to see you here all alone."

He glanced around the table. "I'm not lonely. I have my family."

"Yes, but it's different when you have that special someone with you."

Danielle's image was all he could think about. He halfheartedly tried to think about Jessica instead, but he couldn't shake the image of Danielle.

In the week since he'd met Danielle, she'd managed to consume his thoughts. She was the last thing he thought about before he went to sleep and the first thing he thought about when he woke up in the morning. Now he wanted her here with him at his family dinner.

He hadn't brought a girl since Jessica. Hadn't even wanted to.

"Tell me about her," Veronica said.

"Who?"

"The girl who has you preoccupied."

Samuel laughed. "We're just talking."

Grandma patted him on the hand. "That's a good place to start."

Samuel had one more week. Just one more week before he was supposed to be moved to Dallas to start flying for Skye Travels. For Danielle's father.

Talking to the boss's daughter wasn't the smartest thing he could do. The way he wanted to kiss her was definitely off limits.

It would be smart for him to go ahead and move now, before things went any further. To get her out of his mind. So he could at least have a family dinner without her hijacking his thoughts.

It had been bad enough before he'd kissed her. Holding her hair while she was sick. Helping her set up her computer. Taking her to lunch every day. Walking in the park with her. Listening to her talk. Learning that she hoped she never had to drive.

Then there was that kiss. It wasn't like he hadn't thought about kissing her. Oh, he had thought about kissing her plenty.

If only she weren't the boss's daughter, he'd scoop her up so fast, it'd make both their heads spin.

Perhaps Noah would be understanding. What was the worst thing that could happen?

Besides, if anyone was going to be hurt, it would be him. Danielle already had her hooks in him.

He hadn't seen her or talked to her since he'd dropped her off at her apartment yesterday afternoon. Maybe he should see if she was still talking to him before he planned out their future.

24

---

*D*anielle was deep into Photoshopping the photo of Samuel and her. It had been rather odd at first, working with a picture of herself and the guy who sent her heart into overdrive. After a while, though, she had gotten into adding background images and fonts, and it had become just another cover. For the most part. Every now and then, she'd take a moment to relive that kiss.

She hadn't heard from Samuel since he'd walked her to her door Saturday. She hadn't exactly been encouraging. She wouldn't blame him if he didn't come back.

She checked her phone again. No texts.

She could text him, of course, but, again, her mother had trained her well. *If you want the boy, you have to let him pursue you. Chasing is built into their DNA. If there's no chase, there will be no chance for a relationship.*

She'd thought her mother was ridiculously old-fashioned until her stepfather, a psychologist, had reluctantly agreed with her. Their situation was a little different because they'd dated in high school, but he agreed that he'd never once stayed with a girl who pursued him.

So Danielle sat on her hands and waited. Samuel seemed like an old-fashioned kind of guy, so it didn't seem odd to follow her mother's code with him.

She glanced up with a smile on her face when someone knocked on the door. It was time for Samuel to show up so they could go to lunch.

It wasn't Samuel at her door.

It was Joey.

She hadn't been sick all morning. In fact, she was thinking that maybe she'd gotten over whatever it was that she had. But seeing Joey standing in her doorway had her gauging how quickly she could get to the trashcan.

"Hey Danielle," he said.

She didn't answer.

"I just wanted to bring by your birthday present."

"Birthday present?" She scowled at him.

"Yeah. I had gotten this for you and thought I'd drop it by."

He set a blue gift bag on her desk.

"My birthday was last week."

"I couldn't remember exactly when it was."

Danielle folded her arms. The home pregnancy test had been inconclusive – a complete waste of time and money. *I pray that I'm not pregnant. If I am... and the father of my child doesn't even know when my birthday is...* She reined in her thoughts. "I can't accept it." She put her attention back on her computer. She stared at it, unseeing. Joey had interrupted her whole chain of creativity.

"Okay," he shifted his feet. "I'll just leave it anyway, since I bought it special for you. Do you want to get something to eat?"

She looked back up at him. "No. Joey. I do not want to get something to eat with you. I want you to leave and never come back."

"Surely, you don't mean that. We go way back."

"We may go way back, but we aren't going forward."

"Can't we at least be friends?" He gave her that smile that he used when he was trying to be charming.

"I don't want to be your friend. I don't want you in my life."

He held up a hand. "Okay. Don't get all riled up."

She shook her head. She wasn't *riled* up. She was just feeling quite firm on not wanting Joey anywhere near her.

She pointed to the door. "Go."

"Alright," he said, backing out.

As she watched him leave, she saw him pass Samuel in the open lobby. She still felt nauseated, but she could tell it was different. It really was from seeing her ex.

"Who was that?" Samuel glanced over his shoulder. "Never mind. That was your ex, wasn't it?"

"Is it that bad that you can tell?"

"You look like you're going to be sick."

"I just might."

"What's this?" Samuel pointed to the bag Joey had left on her desk.

Danielle rolled her eyes. "I don't know. He said it was a birthday present."

"A little late for that."

"I know. Right?"

"What is it?" He peeked inside.

"I don't know. I told him I didn't want it."

"Mind if I look?"

"You can have it."

"I doubt that." He pulled out a robe.

Danielle groaned. "Seriously? He brought me a robe? Here." She held out her hand and took the thin robe in her hands. "Old Navy," she said, checking the tag.

Samuel scoffed. "You don't wear Old Navy."

She laughed. And in that moment, it was determined. Her moratorium was over. She was crushing hard on Samuel

Johnson and could no longer punish him just because he came into her life after Joey was in it. He'd known her all of one week and already he knew more about her than her ex-boyfriend ever did.

"I'm glad you're here." She handed the robe back to Samuel.

He stuffed it back in the gift bag. "Why? So I can get rid of this thing? What would you like me to do with it?"

She shrugged, a smile playing about her lips. "Trash can is back here."

He balled up the bag and deftly tossed it in.

"Good shot."

"I'm more than just a pretty face for your novel covers," he said.

Danielle laughed.

"When do I get to see?"

She minimized the cover she was working on and pulled the photo before sliding the computer around so he could see. "Here's the photo I picked."

"Wow," he breathed.

"Here are the other pictures." She scrolled through the photos.

"Can I get a copy of those?"

"Really?"

"Yeah. I've never been in a photo shoot before. And I've definitely never been photographed while kissing. It's kinda... um..."

Danielle smiled. "I know. It's hard to describe, huh?"

"That's an understatement."

She sent copies of the pictures – the dozen or so that she'd picked out to keep herself - to his cell phone. "There you go."

His phone chimed. "Thanks. Let me know when I can see the cover."

"I will. Even if this author doesn't want it, I'll definitely be able to sell it."

"I'm glad I could help out."

"I've never been on a cover either. It's weird."

"Does this author sell a lot?"

Danielle shrugged. "Moderate. Not a name you would recognize, but she does okay."

"Just curious how many people will see us."

"Women all over the world will be swooning over our cover."

He laughed. "You're feeling better today?"

"Yeah," she blew her bangs out of her eyes with a sigh of relief. "I think I may be over what it was I had."

He raised an eyebrow, but didn't say anything. He sat in the chair on the other side of her desk and stretched his long legs out. Then he grinned at her.

She grinned back, and a little shiver traveled down to her toes. Her hands trembled a little, so she put them in her lap. "What?" She asked.

"I love watching you work."

She lowered her eyes. She lifted her fingers to the keyboard, then put them back in her lap and looked up at him. "I don't think I can work with you watching me."

"We could... do something else."

His words sent her thoughts down a very naughty path. Very bad. She replayed the kiss they had shared on Saturday. "Like what?"

He glanced at his watch. "We could get some lunch."

Relief and disappointment washed over her. "Okay."

"You might want to bring your coat," he nodded toward her coat hanging on the coat rack. "The temperature's dropping today."

"Really?" Her face brightened. "Maybe it'll snow."

He laughed. "Not likely, love. This is Houston."

As she reached for her coat, the bottom fell out of her

stomach. *Love?* Surely she heard him wrong. He took her coat and helped her into it.

Pulling her hair from the collar and letting it fall down her back, she smiled into his eyes. He was looking at her now with an intensity she hadn't seen with him before. She licked her lips.

"You're beautiful," he ran his thumb beneath her chin and she trembled. She longed to feel his lips on hers again.

Her phone vibrated in her pocket. She pulled it out. "It's Dr. Neal."

"That was quick," he took a step back, but kept his eyes on hers while she talked.

Danielle listened to the nurse, thanked her, then put the phone back in her pocket.

"I'm pregnant."

25

A host of unexpected emotions washed through Samuel. The first thought was that he had been right. The second was an image of Joey walking past him in the lobby. That led to a wash of anger.

Then came a stab of regret. He wanted to be the father of Danielle's child.

He quickly set aside his own emotions and put his focus back on Danielle. Her face was blank.

"You knew." Her voice was quiet.

He shrugged. "Sisters." He drew her to him into a hug and tucked her head beneath his chin. He held her tightly, and she clung to him. They stood that way in silence as the seconds passed.

He had one week. One week before he had to move to Dallas. He had an apartment reserved with Air BNB for the next two weeks. He wasn't ready to commit to a lease in Dallas. He knew nothing about the city – which area was best to live in. Which area would be a peaceful commute to the airport.

In one week, he would be leaving Danielle on her own, to face an unexpected pregnancy with a man she no longer wanted in her life. He needed to talk to her. To find out what she wanted.

"Come on. Let's get out of here." He took her hand and led her out of her office, through the lobby to the elevator.

They went outside and got into his truck without talking. He didn't ask, he just drove to Pappa's. They were early, so they took a quiet booth in the back.

"How do you feel?" He asked, prepared to get crackers.

"I don't feel sick at the moment. I haven't all morning."

"That's got to be a good thing."

"You have no idea how miserable it is. And humiliating."

"Danielle." He held out his hand and she put hers in his. Their fingers locked loosely. "What do you want to do?"

Her eyes widened. "You mean, do I want to have the baby?"

"Do you?" He couldn't begin to imagine what it would be like to carry the child of someone he didn't love.

She took a deep breath. Looked around and squared her shoulders. "Yes."

He nodded. "Okay then." If she could deal with it, then he would learn to accept it. No matter the biological father, the baby would still be hers.

She pulled her hand away and pressed her fingertips against her forehead. "I have to tell my parents."

He nodded.

"I may not survive that."

He chuckled. "They're your parents. Surely, they'll understand."

"My father, yes. My mother, not so much. Image is very important to her. I'm going to be a disappointment." She was quiet for a moment. "Maybe I should have an abortion."

"Danielle." She looked at him. "Do not have an abortion because you might embarrass your parents."

She shuddered out a breath. "You're right. My mother is coming for a visit this week. I'll get it over with. Actually, it's really convenient that I live here. None of her associates in L.A. have to even know."

"It's hard to hide a child forever."

"Not forever. Just long enough for them to get used to the idea."

"It's a lot for you to get used to, too."

"Yeah. I never saw myself being a single mom."

"You should meet my sister. She's a single mom."

"Your parents were okay with that?"

"They were a little worried at first, you know, but we pitched in to help her out until she got it figured out. She's a great mom."

"You seem very proud of her."

"I am. I admire her."

Their lunch came and they ate in silence for a few minutes.

"I don't know anything about babies," Danielle blurted.

"Nobody does until they have one."

"No. I mean I know zero. I never babysat. No nieces or nephews." She drew a horizontal line with her hand. "Nothing."

"You can take a class or read online." He sipped his soda. Then jumped in with both feet. "Or I can teach you."

She was silent for a few minutes. He didn't know what to expect. "Okay."

He smiled. That meant she was willing to consider having him around after the baby was born.

He took her hand again. "I want to be there for you Danielle."

"Why? Why would want to be there for me when I'm carrying another man's baby?" She lowered her voice to a whisper and gripped his hand.

"Am I the only one feeling a connection here?"

Her lips turned up into a slow smile. "No." Her voice was soft, and her eyes conveyed more than she could know.

"Good." He pulled back and pushed his plate away. "Take a

deep breath, Danielle. Everything is going to work out." Even as he said the words, he knew they were for him.

He was going down a path he'd only been down once before. A path he had sworn he would never go down again. Last time, with Jessica, he'd had it all planned out. This time, he was taking it day by day.

He'd just committed to be there for Danielle when he was going to be in Dallas.

He was going to be doing a lot of flying.

anielle picked at her food. Her mind was going nine million miles an hour.

A baby.

Before last Friday, the whole idea of having a baby was so far off her radar, that world didn't even exist.

Now, in just the span of one week, she'd gone from a girl on a dating moratorium to a pregnant girl with a guy who wanted to connect with her. A guy whose kiss she couldn't get out of her mind. And on top of all that, said guy was a pilot. And Danielle had sworn she would never ever get involved with a pilot. Again.

Yet here he was. The man of her fantasy world sitting in front of her. Kind. Gentle. Attentive. Understanding.

A pilot.

Fate had a sense of humor.

She would never have an abortion. The idea of a life growing inside of her was the strangest and most wonderful feeling she'd ever had. Even if Joey was the sperm donor.

And that, she vowed, was how she was going to think of him from now on.

Samuel had said she needed to tell him about the baby. As far as she was concerned, he'd lost that right when he'd cheated on her.

The baby was hers. And she wasn't going to share it with anyone else.

Well… maybe Samuel.

27

*S*amuel left Danielle at her office with a promise to go to her apartment after work. It would be the first time he'd been inside, and in the evening too. Progress.

It turned out Danielle's mother wasn't the only person coming into town that week.

After he dropped Danielle off at her office, he was headed out to do some errands when he got a text from his boss.

Do you have time to meet in about an hour?

Samuel laughed. When Noah put someone on the payroll, he really expected them to be available.

He sent back a quick answer in the affirmative. A couple of quick texts, and they agreed on a place to meet not far from where Samuel was now.

He ordered a coffee and took a seat in the back of the Starbucks to wait for Noah. Noah was no doubt here to see his daughter and would see her later. A man like Noah would certainly not fly from Dallas to Houston, then drive an hour to meet with an employee who was on the payroll but not yet doing much other than check in on his daughter "now and then." Unless Danielle had told him, he wouldn't know that "now and then" was much more.

And if Samuel had his way, that much more would continue to grow. The problem was going to be all about location. Samuel was falling hard and fast for Danielle, and he wasn't about to let logistics get in his way.

Samuel recognized Noah the minute he walked into the door. Noah Worthington wore success like others wore an old t-shirt. He wore it confidently and barely seemed to notice it was there. Samuel stood up. Noah waved, ordered a coffee, then sat across from Samuel.

Noah was a busy man and didn't mince words. Apparently there were two things he was interested in. "Will you be moved and ready to go to work next Monday?"

Samuel nodded. "I plan to drive up Saturday." He was really thinking Sunday, but he didn't want to sound like he was breezing into town at the last minute for his new job.

Noah waved him off. "I'll send someone down to fly you up."

"My truck…"

"I'll take care of it."

"Alright," Samuel said. So much for his plan to slide into Dallas Sunday. One less day to spend with Danielle.

As though he read his mind, Noah asked his next question. "How's my daughter?"

She's going to have a baby. I think I love her. "She's good."

"You said you were driving her to an appointment last week."

"And I did."

Noah sat back and seemed to relax. "She needs to move New York where driving isn't required."

"Why won't she drive?"

"I don't even know if she knows. She just never had any interest in it. It's almost un-American."

"It's very unusual." Samuel agreed.

"You've been driving her around a lot?"

Samuel nodded.

"And after this week, you won't be here."

Samuel wasn't sure how to respond. Noah stated exactly what Samuel had been wondering. Also, Noah had no idea how much more she was going to need him as her pregnancy progressed. Surely, Danielle would tell him soon. It was a difficult secret to keep, especially with Noah's pointed questions.

"I'll have to think about that," Noah sipped his coffee and after his phone chimed, sent a quick text. "My wife, Savannah."

Samuel smiled. Danielle had spoken fondly of Savannah. Apparently, Savannah was the one person, other than Danielle, that Noah would walk on water for.

"Are you seeing Danielle today?" This conversation would be so much easier if Noah already knew Danielle's circumstance. "I saw her at lunch, and she didn't mention it."

Noah smiled sheepishly. "I had some time, so I thought I'd pop in and surprise her."

"Ah." Noah couldn't have picked a worse day to pop in unannounced. Unless... it was possible that they were close, and she could use the support. Maybe it would be good for her to go ahead and tell Noah.

Not my business.

"I'm gonna go ahead and line you up with some flights for next week."

"Sounds good."

"See you Monday morning. I'll email your itinerary for the week." Noah stood up. Held out his hand.

The two men shook hands, and Noah looked him in the eye. "Don't let me down."

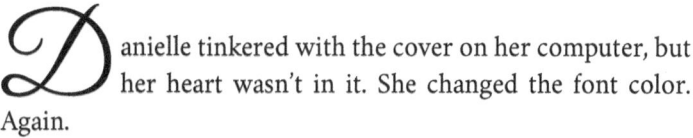anielle tinkered with the cover on her computer, but her heart wasn't in it. She changed the font color. Again.

She was going to have a baby. With Jo... with a sperm donor. Joey wasn't bad-looking, and was smart enough. He didn't read a lot, but he was quick with math. If he'd gone to college, he could have gotten a degree in engineering easily.

And she knew his parents. They were good people. No diseases as far as she knew. So decent genes on his side.

She sighed. If only she carried Samuel's child. They would have beautiful children.

She fiddled with the placement of the author's name, her mind racing with about a million things. She would prefer to tell her father first, but since she needed to do it in person, it looked like her mother was up first.

Maybe she should move back to L.A. to be near her mother. But she had a nice apartment here and a job that she liked. She was left alone to be creative in her own space. Some of the more seasoned cover artists worked from home, so maybe she could do that after the baby came.

She would have to get baby furniture. She needed to look into classes to learn about caring for an infant, much less a child.

Samuel would know. Samuel had nieces and nephews. He knew how to take care of a baby, and he'd offered to help out. But Samuel was going to be in Dallas. Her father lived in Alabama and ran a business based in Fort Worth. Somehow, he managed it, but he mostly supervised the other pilots now. He only did a few contract flights himself. Most of his flying was between Auburn and Fort Worth, and L.A. to see her, until she'd moved. He hadn't been to see her since she moved to Houston. In fact, she had been a little nervous about telling him that she had moved here, much less followed Joey here, but now there was so much more to tell him.

She missed her father terribly.

She could drive up with Samuel this weekend and fly back. She checked the calendar. She'd have to ask off for Monday.

Her head jerked up at three knocks on her door. After Joey showed up unannounced, she was wary of anyone coming to her door unannounced.

Noah stood leaning against the door jamb watching her. "Daddy!" She cried and ran to throw herself in his arms.

Hugged close and safe to her father, she started to cry.

"Hey," Noah said, rubbing her back. "What's this?"

Her breath hitched. "I just haven't seen you in so long. It seems like... so much has happened."

"Besides breaking up with Joey? Has Samuel been helping you out?"

"Samuel. Yes." She wiped at her eyes. "Wait. You knew about Joey?"

"Of course I knew about it."

Danielle sighed. "I was so worried about telling you."

He took her chin in his hand. "Danielle, don't ever be afraid to tell me anything. You know that right? After all we've been through?"

"Of course, Daddy." All those months of counseling. "It's just. It was such a big move. To come here to be with Joey, and it didn't last."

"Speaking of-- Can you leave? Can we get out of here? I'd like to see your apartment."

She snagged a Kleenex from her desk and wiped at her eyes. "Sure. Do you have a car?"

Noah laughed. "Of course I have a car."

Danielle gathered up her things and together they went downstairs, and he followed her directions to her apartment.

"This looks like a nice area." Noah commented as he pulled into her apartment complex.

"I like it." She bit her lip. She did like her apartment and had just gotten moved in and gotten it set up just the way she liked it. She was proud of her apartment and was comfortable here. No. She decided right then. She would stay here. She could raise her baby here.

Once inside, Noah walked around and stuck his head in each of her three bedrooms. Checked out her huge walk-in closet, and came back to the living area. "Nice," he said. "Now come here and tell me what's bothering you."

He sat on the sofa and patted the seat next to him. She sat next to him and took deep calming breaths. Daddy had been through intense therapy with her. She could tell him anything. Right?

"Daddy."

Noah rubbed her back. "You can tell me anything, Princess."

She looked up and stared into her father's loving eyes. Her breath hitched out. "I'm pregnant."

She watched as a range of emotions washed over his face in a matter of seconds. Then he pulled her to him and hugged her again. "It's okay, baby."

"I'm so sorry to disappoint you." She breathed against his chest.

"You could never disappoint me. Never. No matter what you ever do."

She wiped at her eyes.

"Is it… Joey's?"

She rolled her eyes. "He's now referred to as 'the sperm donor'."

"Got it. How do you feel?"

"Better today. I've had morning sickness all day long, every day."

"How did you stand it?"

"Samuel brought me crackers." She laughed. "Oddly enough, it really helped."

"Samuel's been taking care of you."

"I really like him."

"Like him, like him?"

She smiled. "Yeah. I do."

Noah rubbed his eyes with his palms. "That explains it."

"Explains what?"

He looked at her. "I saw Samuel earlier today."

"When? Why?"

"I'm paying him, remember?" Noah had a lopsided grin on his face.

"Right. And you're taking him away. To Dallas."

"Fort Worth."

"Whatever."

Noah laughed. "Working in a different city doesn't mean it can't work. It's a lot harder though."

"I don't even know what we're going to do about it." She said as her phone chimed. "I forgot." She looked up at Noah. "He's supposed to be coming over tonight."

"Okay," Noah said, but she could see the disappointment in his face.

"I'll cancel with him. He's knows you're here, so he'll understand."

"Savannah keeps telling me I need to stop showing up places unannounced."

"It's okay, Daddy. It's who you are."

He grinned. "You, on the other hand, take after your mother in all the good ways."

"You mean, I call before I show up?"

"It's a good quality to have."

"What do you think Mom's gonna think? About the baby?"

Noah shook his head. "I don't know. She's a lot different now that she's with Grayson."

"She's coming here in two days."

"That doesn't give you much time with Samuel, does it? Between the two of us."

"It's okay. I'm supposed to be in a dating moratorium anyway."

"Who said that?"

"It's self-imposed."

Noah stood up and paced to the window where she had a nice view of the pool. "Want some fatherly advice?"

"Always."

"I don't know Samuel very well, but he seems like a nice guy. His background checked out." He looked at her sheepishly. "I like him well enough to hire him. If you like him, you shouldn't let what happened with J…"

"Sperm donor."

"Right. You shouldn't let what happened with 'sperm donor' affect the possibility of a relationship with Samuel."

"That's kind of what I've been telling myself." She got up and went toward the kitchen. "Do you want anything?"

"Just some water." He glanced at his watch. "You know what? If I leave right now, I can make it home in time to have dinner with Savannah."

She handed him the water bottle. "She'd like that."

"But, if it's okay with you, I'd like to come back next week, when Samuel is working, and spend the night. We can talk about what all we need to do to prepare for the baby." A stunned look appeared on his face. "I'm going to be a *grandfather*."

Danielle laughed. "You never thought you'd see the day, did you?

"No. Now I really need to talk to Savannah. She can talk me down off the cliff."

"Daddy, it's okay. You'll be the youngest and coolest grandfather ever."

"I love you, little one."

"I love you too, Daddy. I'm so glad you came by."

After Noah left, Danielle sent a text back to Samuel. *Daddy left already. You can still come at seven.*

That gave her three hours to take a long hot bath and figure out something to cook.

29

*S*amuel stood at the flower shop in Kroger and shifted from one foot to the other. He hadn't come to buy flowers. He stopped in to get deodorant, but the flowers had gotten his attention.

He hadn't had a date since Jessica. The only flower he ever took Jessica was actually a plant, an ivy. She didn't like girly things, and Samuel had picked up pretty quickly that she wouldn't appreciate a flower that would last no more than a few days.

Danielle, however, was the complete opposite. In fact, he thought wryly, he could almost go with the exact opposite of anything he'd done with Jessica.

Roses seemed too formal. This wasn't a formal date. It was just a couple of friends getting together. Friends who were moving toward something else, but weren't quite there yet. It would be nice to have a playbook – a place where he could look up the appropriate thing at each stage in a relationship. It would be especially helpful if there was a section on *what to do if your girlfriend is already pregnant.*

He looked at every flower in the shop. Then he went back

to the one that had gotten his attention when he was just walking by. It was a little bouquet of white daisies. It looked fresh and happy. Simple and uncomplicated.

Making a decision, he took it to the woman behind the desk and asked her to wrap it up for him.

He left Kroger happily with deodorant and flowers, heading home for a quick shower before he went to Danielle's apartment.

As he was heading to what he referred to as his apartment behind the house, his mother came out the back door and stood on the deck. "Samuel."

He stopped. Busted.

"Is there something you haven't told us?" His mother asked, gesturing toward the flowers.

"They're for a... friend."

"A girl?"

He rolled his eyes. "Really Mom. I wouldn't take flowers to a guy."

"Well, that's just convenient, isn't it? Since you're leaving Sunday."

He sighed. He might as well get the bad news over with. "It got moved to Saturday."

"Then I guess I'll have to ask everyone to come over Friday instead of Saturday."

"Mom, please. Don't invite everyone, wait until the next weekend. I'll come back, and I'll have something to talk about."

"Too late."

"I wanted to just have a nice quiet evening at home."

"You have to bring her."

He was already shaking his head. "I can't do that. I actually like this girl."

"I kinda thought you did, since this is the first girl I've known you to show any interest in since... in quite a long time."

Samuel sighed. His family was still tiptoeing around talking about Jessica's death. Maybe it was time to give them someone else to talk about. "Okay, Mom. I'll make you a deal."

"What deal is that?"

"Leave off the party this weekend, and I'll bring her by to meet everyone the first weekend I'm back in town."

Minutes later, with the hot water running over his head, Samuel found his thoughts again consumed by Danielle. He replayed that kiss again in his head. He'd played it a hundred times in last two days. He wanted more.

It was time to move their relationship from the friend zone and to build upon the foundation they'd established with that kiss from heaven.

30

*I*t felt a little strange having Samuel there in her apartment.

The white daisies, she'd put in a vase in the center of the dining room table; they brightened the whole room. He'd brought her the perfect flowers. She smiled as she put on an oven mitt and slipped the lasagna back into the oven. It was just one of many hot dishes her mother had taught her to throw together in a few minutes. She'd put it together and left it covered in the refrigerator until she made sure Samuel was planning to eat with her.

She looked across the counter, past the dining room table, to the living room, where she'd left Samuel with her laptop.

He'd asked to look at some of the covers she'd created, so she'd opened a file for him to look at while she checked the lasagna in the oven.

Every nerve was on edge having him here in her apartment. They hadn't called it a date, but it sure felt like one.

As she watched, he set the computer on her coffee table and walked toward her to the kitchen. She smiled and turned.

"Tomorrow, I get to cook."

"Tomorrow?"

"I have to leave Saturday." He stepped closer until he was close enough to touch her. "And I want to see you every day."

"Is that so?" She asked.

"And every night."

She backed up until she bumped against the counter. He placed his hands on each side of her, pinning her in front of him.

Her breath hitched at the intensity of his gaze. She'd seen that look in the photos they'd taken when he was about to kiss her. She hadn't seen it then because her eyes had been closed.

She had dated a lot of guys, but she couldn't remember any of them ever looking at her quite like this.

Without touching anywhere else, he placed his lips against hers, ever so lightly. Then he leaned back enough to smile into her eyes.

Her heart flip-flopped, and she smiled back.

His grin turning devilish, he reached down, put an arm beneath her knees, and picked her up. She squeaked and threw her arms around his neck. He carried her as though she was light as a feather to the sofa. He sat down with her in his lap.

Her heart was racing ninety to nothing as he put his lips against the corner of her mouth and a hand behind her head to hold her close.

He tasted minty. She recognized the faint smell of his cologne. His lips sent tingles all through her, and she wanted his lips on hers.

She turned into the kiss and sighed when he pressed his lips against hers. This. This was what she'd been craving since that kiss two days ago. Only now, without anyone watching through a camera lens, it was even better than she'd remembered.

His fingers threaded through her hair as he moved his lips against hers. She never wanted to stop. Ever.

They kissed until the timer on the stove went off. He pulled back and ran a finger along her swollen lips.

It was almost perfect. If only she dated pilots.

31

They sat on the sofa and ate with their thighs and shoulders touching. Samuel didn't want to let go of her.

Though she wasn't physically pulling away, she hadn't made eye contact since they'd stopped kissing.

"Alright. What's wrong?" He asked.

She smiled. "It's just something I have to work out."

"Maybe I can help, since I have a feeling it involves me in some way."

"You won't like it."

"Maybe I can change it."

She laughed. "Okay, but don't say I didn't warn you."

"Duly warned."

"I don't date pilots."

"Me either," he said without a hitch.

She stared at him. Then took another bite of pasta. Then she chuckled. "You're a pilot."

"This is really good," he said as he filled his fork. "Don't think of me as a pilot."

"Okay… What should I think of you as?"

"Anything. Think of me as your yard boy."

She laughed. "Why would I need a yard boy? I live in an apartment."

"I'm sure you can think of something for me to do. As your yard boy, I can run errands. I'm really good at running errands. I even do returns."

"What about when you're off flying a plane?"

"Just a taxi driver. Not a pilot." He winked at her and nudged her shoulder with his. At least she was looking at him again.

"I'm serious." She insisted.

"So am I." He set his empty plate on the coffee table.

"Just because you don't call yourself a pilot, doesn't mean you aren't one."

"And just because I'm a pilot, doesn't mean you shouldn't date me."

She shot him a look of fake exasperation.

"What do you have against pilots anyway?" He tucked a strand of hair behind her ear.

"They're always away. Remember, I have first-hand experience as the daughter of a pilot."

"A famous pilot."

"I don't know about famous, but definitely successful."

"In the pilot world." He lifted one eyebrow. "He's a famous pilot. So besides being gone a lot, what else do you have against my breed?"

She pulled her feet under her and hugged a pillow to her. "Pilots aren't... monogamous."

"What? Really? Why am I just now learning about this?" He feigned shock.

She chuckled. "It's the stewardesses. They're like candy for y'all."

"Oh, well, you're doubly safe. They don't have stewardesses anymore, only flight attendants. And I don't eat candy."

"You don't eat candy. Ever?"

"Never."

"What about a brownie?"

He shook his head. "No sweets for me, unless I'm with you." He leaned back and put an arm across the back of the sofa. "So, if I'm a taxi driver by day and your yard boy by night, does that grant me exception status?"

"I'll have to think about it."

"What if I promise to send you flowers every day?"

"Now you're just teasing me."

"How about if I drive you around, and you never have to drive or take other transportation?"

"But you're not here, remember?"

"Oh right. Then when I'm here. And don't forget, I do errands."

"I'll have to get back to you. What else do you have to offer?"

"I can do foot rubs."

"Really? I might have to see if you're any good."

"Ah. I can offer a free sample right now. If you want."

"Sure. I never turn down a foot massage."

"Here." He held out his hand. She shifted her feet toward him. He took her shoe off and put her foot across his knees. She leaned back against the pillows. He started with her toes and worked his way to the bottom of her feet to her ankles. She had adorable red toenails.

She closed her eyes, and he moved to the other foot.

He shifted to pull her toward him, holding her close. "I also offer unlimited heavenly kisses." He whispered against her ear before claiming her mouth again.

_____

32

The next morning, Danielle managed to stay focused enough to get a draft of the cover she was working on ready to send to the author.

She held her breath as she emailed it. It had a completely different couple on it from what they agreed on. Danielle wasn't sure what she was going to do if the author asked for the original couple. It was a good thing she hadn't posted her picture on Facebook or the company website. She'd prefer that no one know that she was the girl on the cover.

She was watching the door more than she was watching her computer as she scrolled through a website looking at potential images to make a premade cover.

The minute he stepped off the elevator, she saw him. Her heart rate increased to dangerous levels, and she stared at her computer screen so he wouldn't know she was watching for him.

He pulled off his sunglasses and grinned at her. Her heart melted. He hadn't shaved today, so he had a bit of a shadow on his face. She wanted to run her hands along his cheeks to see what it felt like.

Instead of sitting across from her like he usually did, he walked up to her and kissed her right on the lips. "Hi," he pulled a white rose from behind his back and handed it to her.

"Hi." She gazed at him, unable to think. She sniffed the rose and held it next to her cheek.

"What are you working on?" Apparently, he didn't have the same problem with his thought processes.

"Oh, I um… I finished the cover."

"Can I see?"

She opened the file and pulled the cover up on her screen.

He studied it with a ridiculous grin on his face. "We look good," he said. "And the cover is nicely done, too. I'm impressed."

"Thanks. I just hope the author likes it. This one's a little more personal."

"So the author won't know it's you?"

"I hope not."

"That's probably good. Avery was right. We look like we need to get a room."

Danielle laughed. She could see it, too. Then she gasped. "Oh no."

"What is it?"

"My colleagues are going to see it." She nodded toward her door leading to the other offices.

He seemed unconcerned. "They might want to hire us as models. It could open a whole new career for you."

She patted her stomach. "I think not."

"Right. Well, you won't be pregnant forever."

"Are you sure?" It seemed like it was all she could think about.

"Do you want the usual for lunch?"

"Do you mind terribly?"

He leaned over and kissed her lightly on the lips. "Your heart's desire is my command."

Taking her hand, he led her through the lobby. It was empty, but it felt like a public announcement that they were seeing each other.

"Did I tell you my mom is coming in tomorrow?"

"You mentioned it," Samuel held the elevator for her. "Did she say how long she'll be staying?"

"Not yet."

"How long does she usually stay?"

"I don't know. She's never visited."

"Really? Never?"

"I lived at home until I moved here."

"Ah." He held the elevator door open when it stopped on the first floor.

"What about you? Where do you live?"

"Similar, I guess. My parents have what I guess you'd call a pool house behind their house. I live in it. It's a little two-room place, but I have privacy. Until now, I was rarely home anyway."

"Right. The whole taxi driver thing."

He grinned and helped her into the truck. "You're a fast learner."

He walked around the truck and got in the driver's seat. "So... do I get to meet her?"

"You want to meet my mom?"

"Why wouldn't I?"

She shrugged.

"Too soon?" He put on his blinker and made a U-turn to get into the Pappa's parking lot.

Danielle laughed. "Maybe."

"Are you going to tell her about the baby?"

"I told my dad, so, yeah, I need to get that over with, too." She bit her lip as she said the words and looked down.

"Want me to be there with you?"

"She might get confused."

"Really? I thought your mom was a successful business owner."

Danielle laughed. "She is. Okay, I might get confused. Or distracted."

He took her hand as they walked into the restaurant. The guy at the counter already knew what they were going to order.

It was crowded today, so they sat across from each other at a small booth for two.

He held out his hand, and she put hers in his.

"You haven't told me anything about your dating history." A shadow crossed his features and wiped away his smile. She immediately wished she could take back the words. "You don't have to talk about it."

"No. It's okay. I'll tell you. It's just not a good story."

"I'm not looking for a good story. I just want to know about you. After all, you kinda know about me." He definitely knew what she'd done with her previous boyfriend.

Samuel smiled again. "You don't have to tell me." His expression growing serious, he took a deep breath and lifted his chin. "Six years ago I met a girl – Jessica. We started dating and got engaged after about two years. Right after that, she was deployed to Afghanistan. She actually did one tour, came home, and had just started her second when she was killed."

Danielle gasped. "Oh no!"

"Yeah. That was two years ago. I haven't dated anyone since."

"I don't know what to say."

He shook his head. "There's nothing to say. She was my only serious girlfriend. So... I don't date. Until you."

Danielle gazed into his eyes and squeezed his hand. This

man who hadn't put himself out there until her. It made it all the more special that he liked her.

"I've gone on lots of dates," she told him, lowering her voice. "But I only slept with two. Scout's honor." She raised her hand and made the Vulcan "V" with her fingers.

He laughed, as was her intent.

"I'm not worried about your past. As far as I'm concerned, we're starting with a clean slate."

"I like that."

Maybe it was time she began thinking of him as a boyfriend.

33

*S*amuel hadn't wanted to tell Danielle about Jessica. He'd wanted to start fresh without bringing that cloud along with him, but it hadn't seemed fair to keep it from her. She needed to know that he could do long-term relationships, and he didn't trifle with girls. Even when he was traveling.

She had been right about pilots, at least some of them. Samuel had heard stories and he'd seen things with his own eyes. Otherwise good men, even some married ones, going home with flight attendants for one-night-stands or even having long-term affairs.

But he didn't do that. Still, it would be a hard thing to prove. Traveling so much made trust difficult to establish and maintain.

He knew firsthand from both sides. When Jessica was in Afghanistan with the male soldiers, it had been difficult. They'd gotten through it by constantly staying in touch with daily phone calls and emails.

He had some time to kill after an appointment out toward Katy, so he stopped back by the Memorial City Mall and walked aimlessly waiting for the time to pass until he could see Danielle again. He wanted to get her something for the baby. He wanted to be the first person to give her a gift. Had she even thought about decorating the baby's room yet?

She'd had so much to process in such a short time, it probably hadn't even occurred to her yet. A baby gift would open the door to allow him to offer to help her decorate.

He hoped she would find out ahead of time whether it was a boy or a girl. His older sister had waited to find out, and the whole nursery had been decorated in yellow and green. His younger sister had learned from that and was able to do the room in pink beforehand—a much better choice in Samuel's opinion. Practicality was totally underrated.

He wandered around a bit until he came to a Build-A-Bear shop. He had gotten one for each of his nieces and nephews. Perfect.

He spent the next hour shopping among the store full of mothers and children picking out the perfect teddy bear and outfit for it.

After choosing a dark gray bear, he looked around at outfits until he found a pilot's uniform. Grinning, he picked it up and took it with him. On the way to get the bear stuffed, he passed accessories and snagged a little stuffed camera.

"Do you want to pick a sound?" The girl, not a day over eighteen, asked.

"Sound?"

"We have sounds now. You can pick out whichever one you like." She explained how the kiosk worked and played some of the different sounds for him.

"Can I add one later?"

"Of course."

Next, he had to insert a heart into the back of the bear. Following the lead of a six-year-old, he kissed the little heart and tucked it carefully into the bear's stuffing.

Finally, it was time to create a birth certificate and name the bear. "Cute." The girl commented as she checked him out and tucked the bear into a little box. "Enjoy!"

He was left with just enough time to take a quick shower, stop by the market, and head over to Danielle's.

When she answered the door, she looked different. She was wearing a dark blue sheath dress with navy ankle boots. Besides being dressed up, she looked different.

"Whoa. What's the occasion?"

"Nothing," She tossed her very straight hair.

"Did I forget something?"

"No." She smiled. "I just stopped by the Dry Bar for a blow out."

He followed her inside and she closed the door. "A blow… what?" His mind went down a path he couldn't even follow.

"I had my hair blow-dried."

He reached out to touch a soft strand of hair that lay against her shoulder. "It looks great." He followed her into the kitchen and set down his bags. "You're dressed up."

"Yeah." She ran a hand down her dress. A dress that accented her tiny waist – she wasn't showing yet. "Pretty soon I won't be able to wear these clothes anymore. At least not for a while, so I thought I'd just wear them."

"I thought I'd missed something."

She grinned. "What did you bring?" She peaked in a bag.

"Kale vegetable salad. Since you're eating for two, I thought we'd try Tuesday healthy night."

"That's a great idea." She said.

Except that now that he'd said it out loud, he realized that it was a terrible idea, because next Tuesday he wouldn't be here. Or any Tuesday after that.

Damn. This was not working out like he wanted it to.

He would have to make the most of what he had. "I brought you something." He kept his voice light, despite his sudden despondent mood. "It's for you, but also for the baby."

He brought out the box with the bear and handed it to her.

"Oh! A baby gift. What is it?"

"Open it."

She took it over to the dining room table and examined the air holes in the box. "Is it a kitten?"

He shrugged, and mentally filed away the idea that she might like a kitten.

She opened the box and pulled out the traditional bear that he'd chosen for her. "A teddy bear." Her face exploded into a smile.

"I wanted to be the first person to give the baby a gift." He reached into the box and took out a certificate. "I made it myself and dressed it in the little pilot uniform. And look; it has a camera. And I gave it a name."

She looked at the paper. "You named it Pappa."

"Yeah. For Pappa's Burgers."

Her eyes grew moist.

"What's wrong?" He drew her close and wrapped his arms around her and the bear. "You don't like bears?"

"Nobody ever made a bear for me."

"Oh honey. It's going to be okay."

She pulled back and wiped a tear from her cheek. "It's like a combination of both of us."

He smiled. "I know."

She ran her hand along the bear's fur. "I apologize. I'm not normally this emotional."

"It's to be expected. You have a lot going on. I brought you this too." He reached inside the box and pulled out a baby name book and a yellow highlighter.

"A name. Oh. My. I forgot I had to name it. There's so much to think about."

He chuckled. "That's why I'm here." He took her hand and

led her to the sofa. "You sit here. Put your feet up, and spend some time with this book while I make dinner."

Tomorrow, he would pick up a copy of *What to Expect When You're Expecting.*

The more time he spent with her, the more he knew that he needed to be here with her. Not in Dallas. Not flying people around the country.

What kind of spell had she cast over him to make him want to stay on the ground and out of the sky?

34

$\mathcal{T}$he next morning, Danielle put on some leggings and a sweater dress. Her mother was coming in sometime that afternoon, so she wanted to be presentable. She also liked the reaction she got from Samuel when she'd dressed up.

They'd had a surprisingly good kale salad with lots of different vegetables, then sat talking on the sofa for a while, looking at some of the names she'd highlighted. They'd ended up kissing until midnight. Samuel declared that he would not be responsible for her turning into a pumpkin.

"Cinderella doesn't turn into a pumpkin."

"Well, something does, and I won't be responsible."

She walked him to the door in her bare feet, then kept his lips on hers for another twenty minutes before she told him to get out so she could get some sleep.

As a result, she was a little tired today. Her mother was planning to only stay one night, so Samuel was going to be on standby, but the plan was for them to skip tonight.

That meant they only had three more evenings together. She thought several times about calling and asking her mother to wait until next week to visit, but her mother wouldn't show up without a good reason.

She took an Uber to work as always and was absorbed in her work when Samuel showed up at her door.

"Is it noon already?"

"I'm early. I wanted to give you this." He handed her a book about being pregnant.

"I never even thought about getting a book. I seriously don't know what I'm going to do without you."

He hadn't answered her, but instead had helped her into her coat. "My younger sister has a copy with highlights and color-coded tabs."

"I am not that organized."

"Creative people usually aren't." They headed toward the elevator. "The usual?"

"You know what? About that-- I was thinking maybe we could have Mexican instead."

His face lit up. "I know just the place."

Relief washed over her. She'd been reluctant to change their lunch spot since he'd gone to the trouble to get her a teddy bear and even named it Pappa. Technically, she supposed he'd gotten it for the baby. But still...

When they were seated at the restaurant, she asked something she'd been curious about. "So technically, you're working for my father right now?"

"Yeah. He's paying me for two weeks to pack and relocate."

"But are you? Relocating?"

"No. I'm keeping my house, and I've rented an Air BNB in Dallas for the next two weeks. So it'll be like staying in a hotel."

"So what do you do all day?"

"I spend a lot of time with you."

She smiled. "Other than that."

"I actually am packing and doing errands. One of my specialties, if you recall."

She nodded.

"And I've met with two people about an airplane."

"An airplane? What do you mean?"

"I'm looking into buying a small airplane."

"Wow. You haven't mentioned that."

"Yeah. I haven't decided for sure that I'm going to do it. It's a big investment. I'm not even sure that I'll have time to use it after I go to work for your father. It's my understanding that he keeps his pilots flying four to five days a week."

"Huh." There were so many implications in what he had just said that she needed to process everything."

"I wouldn't be able to buy it outright." He clarified. "I'd have to borrow most of the money, so I've met with a couple of banks, too."

"You've been busy."

"Yeah. I'm not fond of driving. I mean I don't mind driving around Houston at all. But I really try to avoid driving long distances. And with my family here, I'd like to be able to get here quickly and often. It's something I've been thinking about since I took the job with your dad. Then this week, I really started to take some steps to make it happen."

"Since it's getting closer to time for you to leave."

"Yeah. That and you."

Me. Did that mean he wanted to be able to continue to spend time with her? There was a big difference in driving from Fort Worth and flying.

Of course, after he rented a car and drove from the airport, the time would probably just about equal out.

Danielle received a message on her phone. "I think it's the author."

"She's just now responding?"

"I think she's had the flu or something." She read the message, then passed her phone over for Samuel to read it.

"She loves it." Danielle nearly bounced in her chair.

"She said she's never seen such chemistry portrayed on a cover."

"She likes it."

"We should celebrate," Samuel said. "How about a strawberry lemonade?"

Danielle laughed with a burst of happiness. She had a happy customer and a handsome boyfriend who celebrated with her by buying her lemonades at lunch.

She'd always heard that it was the little things that make people happy.

35

Claire Beauchamp Worthington Moore arrived at Danielle's apartment in a limo. She stepped out wearing a black sheath dress with a short black jacket and black pumps with red bottoms.

Danielle watched from the window as her mother waited for the limo driver to unload her luggage. She took out her phone, and Danielle's rang.

"Hi Mom."

"Where are you?"

"I'll be right there." Danielle smiled and went out her door and hugged her mom.

Claire pushed back and, putting her hands on the sides of Danielle's face, examined her daughter. "You look good."

"Thanks. So do you. Come on in."

Claire motioned for the limo driver to bring her luggage, and they followed Danielle into her apartment.

Much as her father had done, Claire walked through the apartment and gave her nod of approval. "Nice place."

"Thanks. I like it here."

"Do you want to get dinner?"

"Sure." Danielle opened her phone. "We'll have to get a taxi." Her mother didn't use Uber.

"The limo driver is waiting. Do you know a good place?"

"There's a nice Italian place nearby."

She climbed into the limo and sat next to her mother. "How long do you have the limo?" Danielle asked.

"Just tonight. It's a long way down here from the airport."

Half an hour later, when they were seated at a table, Claire ordered a club soda instead of her usual red wine.

Following her mother's lead, Danielle ordered the same.

Claire was quiet, but she fidgeted with her napkin, her fork, and finally leaned forward. "I have to tell you something."

"I have something to tell you, too."

"Okay."

"You first," Danielle said. Her mother looked like she was about to burst.

"Okay I'll go first. Danielle, I'm pregnant."

Danielle stared at her mother, who was obviously ecstatic. "Wow."

"I know. Grayson and I are so excited. I wanted to come and tell you in person."

"How far along are you?"

"About seven weeks."

Close to where Danielle was. Surely this was not happening. "I don't know what to say."

"I know it's unexpected."

"I'm happy for you." Danielle hoped she sounded happier than she felt.

"What did you want to tell me?"

Danielle couldn't do it. She couldn't tell her. She couldn't risk taking that ecstatic grin off her mother's face by shocking her mother. Claire, after all, was happily married.

"I have a new boyfriend." She blurted.

36

"How did it go with your mom?" Samuel stretched out his legs across from Danielle's desk. He'd brought them coffee from Starbucks – hers a caffeine-free latte. It was early, not even nine o'clock, but he'd missed seeing her last night.

"Interesting." She put her elbows on the desk, her brow furrowed.

"Somehow, I have a feeling she didn't take it so well."

Danielle bit her lip. "I didn't tell her."

"Oh. What happened?"

Danielle looked at him for about a minute, then looked down. "She had something to tell me as well."

"It must have been something important."

She took a deep breath and looked back at him. "She's pregnant."

Samuel didn't say anything. He was too stunned.

"I had the same reaction," Danielle said.

"That's got to be… um… kinda weird."

"It's so weird, I can't begin to wrap my head around this."

Samuel laughed. He couldn't help it. "It's not funny."

But then Danielle was laughing with him. "How am I going to tell her?"

Samuel sobered. "We'll fly out and tell her."

"We?"

"Yeah. I'll have my new plane by the end of the week."

"You got it?" She jumped up and ran around to kiss him on the lips. "That is so exciting."

"Exciting and scary all at once."

"I'm so happy for you."

"Do you want to see pictures?"

"Of course." She sat down next to him, and he scrolled through pictures on his phone of the little plane he'd just bought. It had a single black stripe down the tail.

"When are you going to take me up?" She asked.

"Well, it won't be this weekend, but if everything goes as planned, how about the next weekend?"

"Sounds perfect."

He was going to ask her to meet his family that weekend, too, but he wasn't quite ready to broach the subject. They only had two more evenings together, and he didn't want to overwhelm her.

"Do you still want Mexican food?" He asked. "Or are you craving seafood again?"

"Mexican sounds great."

As they sat together on a bench waiting for a table, Samuel reached over and took her hand. He didn't want to leave. He didn't want to leave Houston anyway – his home and family – but he especially didn't want to leave Danielle.

Though it was just under two weeks instead of two years, it was like Jessica all over again. Only this time, he was the one going away. At least he wasn't going to war, and he could come back any time he wanted to.

Danielle reached up and ran a finger between his eyes. "Such deep thoughts."

He turned and looked into her green eyes. "I don't want to leave you."

"But it's exciting to be starting a new job."

He shook his head. "I don't care about the job. I mean, I'm honored to be working with your father, but I'd rather be with you."

She smiled, and he kissed her.

"Since you're not sick any more, do you want to get out and do something tonight? Maybe see a movie?"

37

"I have feeling that's the last time I go out to a movie." Danielle settled on the sofa with Samuel, pulling a blanket over them as he handed her a mug of hot chocolate.

"Why would you say that?" He sipped on his own steaming hot chocolate.

"I had to get up way too many times and go to the restroom." She counted four times. "At least with a movie at home, we can pause it."

He laughed. "Alright. But after the baby comes, you should be good."

"Ha. I think I'll be staying home taking care of said baby for a very long time."

"I don't know." He looked at her sideways. "Aunts and uncles make great built-in babysitters."

"Ah. But I don't have any siblings. Yet. And my one half-sibling is going to be my baby's age, so no babysitters there."

"I, on the other hand, have three."

Danielle lifted an eyebrow. "And that helps me how?" She knew it was a leading question, but she couldn't help herself. Besides, he was the one who brought it up.

"Well, when we want to have a night out, we'll have a babysitter."

"Maybe." Danielle shrugged, but her heart was racing. He was talking many months from now. Was he talking about a long-term commitment?

"Alright." His voice sounded a bit challenging. "Come with me a week from Sunday to lunch. You'll get to meet my whole family, and you'll see that they're babysitter-worthy."

"You want me to meet your family?"

"Lunch is at Pappa's." He added with a grin.

"Well, why didn't you say so?" She picked up the teddy bear that she kept on the sofa. She would never, ever tell him that she had been taking it to bed with her.

"Did I pick out the perfect name for him or what?" Samuel asked, tipping her chin up with a finger to kiss her on the lips.

"Of course you did," she said, handing him her mug to set down. Right now, the only thing sweet she wanted was kissing.

"And speaking of being here." Samuel set their mugs on the coffee table. "I get my plane tomorrow."

"Oh wow. Exciting! Do I get to go see it?"

"You want to?"

"Of course I do."

He wrapped his arms around her and pulled her against him. He kissed her forehead, her eyelids, her cheeks, then finally her lips. By the time his tongue lightly touched the roof of her mouth, she was no longer worried about movies or meeting his family or anything else.

38

---

*S*amuel should have been over the moon excited about getting his plane. It was used, of course, but it was a sleek little Mooney single-engine airplane. They didn't make them like this anymore. The previous owner had painted a black stripe along the tail. Samuel didn't mind. It made it distinctive.

He'd thought about bringing Danielle with him up to see it, but decided he would wait until he came back next week. This was their last evening together, and he wanted it to be special.

He'd made reservations at Masraff's on Post Oak Boulevard, and he'd sent a text asking if she had a formal dress. He'd laughed at her response.

Of course I do. Unfortunately, they're all in LA. Are you giving me an excuse to go shopping?

He written back. *Absolutely!*

How formal?

Black tie.

I'm intrigued.

See you at seven... after lunch.

LOL.

He'd shown her pictures of his plane at their new lunch spot – the Mexican restaurant – and she'd told him about her new client.

He was going to miss their daily lunch date.

As he drove back toward the city, he wondered what Danielle was doing. She'd said she was going to take the afternoon off and go shopping at the Galleria.

His fingers itched to text her. To see if she was safe. He would have gone with her if he hadn't needed the plane for tomorrow. Noah had taken it in stride that he'd be flying himself up.

Leaving her here, pregnant, was going to be difficult. What if something went wrong, and she needed him? What if he was in the air, and she couldn't reach him?

For the hundredth time, he wished he hadn't taken this job. But, damn, it was too good to turn down.

It occurred to him then that Noah didn't know they were in a serious relationship. Danielle had asked him to wait until he'd been working there a bit to tell him. She'd told her mother she had a new boyfriend, but hadn't said he was a pilot, much less Noah's newest employee.

It was going to be difficult. Samuel wanted to tell everyone. Besides, if Noah knew, it might afford him some leeway to visit his daughter. Samuel wasn't above using whatever avenues presented themselves to see her.

Getting the plane had taken longer than he'd expected. He had lots to do in less than three hours.

39

*D*anielle sprayed some perfume in the air and walked through it. She'd gone with classic black. She already had black pumps to go with the dress she'd gotten. The strapless dress fell straight to the floor in a sleek, modern look. Pressing her hand against her stomach, she could feel just a little baby bump. But looking in the mirror, she couldn't see it. She shook her head. It was much too soon. It had to be her imagination.

Nonetheless, a little blip of excitement shot through her, and she couldn't wait to see if Samuel could feel it.

The dress was probably not one of the wisest purchases she'd made. She probably wouldn't wear it but once, and then all bets were off whether or not she would be able to wear it post-baby.

She'd had her hair styled at the Dry Bar. She blamed Savannah, her stepmother for getting her hooked on that luxury. Her sleek hair cascaded around her shoulders. Tonight was the last night she would see Samuel for a whole week.

He wanted it to be special, and she wanted to look her best. At a quarter to seven, she went into her living room and sorted through her mail, cleared off her coffee table, leaving just the baby name book, and paced back to the bedroom. She decided at the last minute to wear her diamond pendant. A gift from her father on her college graduation, it had five small round diamonds sprinkled along a platinum chain.

As she took one last look in the mirror, her doorbell rang. By the time she got to the door on the other end of the apartment, she was a little breathless. She opened the door, and Samuel stood there in a black tux, holding a single red rose.

She stood there a moment, her hand on the doorknob, taking in his handsome smile and letting the warm emotions flow throw her.

"Wow," he said. "You look absolutely stunning."

"You clean up pretty nice yourself." She stepped back, opening the door wide, matching his smile with her own.

He held out the rose, and she took it from him to put in a vase. Before setting it on the counter, she inhaled deeply and ran her fingers along the soft petals. She sighed.

Stay in the moment. He's still here.

She turned brightly and took his hand. "Ready?"

He brought her hand to his lips and kissed her knuckles.

It only took a few minutes to get to Masraff's. "Have you been here?" He asked.

"No." She said as they pulled into the parking lot. Samuel gave the keys to the valet, then came around, helped her out of the truck, and took her hand as they crossed the parking lot.

They were a few minutes early, so they went into the bar and sat near the fireplace. Samuel ordered sparkling water and held up his glass. "To us."

"To us," she repeated as their glasses met in a toast. *Us.* She would have to think about that later.

"It'll be Thanksgiving in a couple of weeks," Samuel said.

"I know. Then Christmas already. Savannah, Noah's wife, is

graduating with her doctorate in a few weeks, so I'll be travelling to Auburn."

"And we have to fly out to see your mother."

"Are we taking your plane?"

He shook his head. "It's too small. I'll probably see if I can use one of your dad's."

Danielle studied the flames in the fireplace. Their lives were quickly becoming enmeshed. She'd gone from not dating anyone to having what looked to be a relationship in a flash.

Samuel took her hand. "Your dad will be alright with us seeing each other, right? I mean, eventually."

"Sure." Her father had always been supportive. He'd always been there for her. Besides, he'd already suggested that she not let her previous relationship disaster prevent her from moving forward with Samuel. Something held her back, though, from telling him that yet.

The hostess appeared at their side and led them to their table.

They ordered crab cakes for an appetizer, and they each ordered the sea bass for their entrée.

Soft music played in the background. Danielle was determined not to let this being their last night together for a week overshadow the moment. Nonetheless, she had to blink back tears before lifting her chin and putting a smile on her face.

"Are you excited?" She tapped a newly-manicured nail against her glass of sparkling water. "About your new job?"

"It'll be good to fly again, but it's hard to be excited when I'll be leaving you."

She sucked in her breath. "I'm not excited about it either."

"You know," he said, lacing his fingers with hers on the table. "We have a good thing here. Do you think?"

She smiled. "I think so, too."

"Danielle, do you want to be my girlfriend?"

She laughed. "You mean like your steady girlfriend?"

"I don't know what they call it now. Exclusive maybe?"

"Whatever they call it, yes."

He leaned over the table and sealed it with a light kiss on her lips. "I'm happy. Are you happy?"

"Yes, but Samuel? Are you sure?" She ran a hand down her stomach. Felt the little baby bump. Later, when he took her home, she would see if he could feel it. "I come as a package."

"I don't mind. In fact, I'm kind of excited about the baby."

She grinned. Life was finally going the right way.

40

*S*amuel wasn't thinking about anything other than spending some quality time with Danielle on her couch. If he'd been clear-headed, he would have seen Joey sitting on the steps leading up to her apartment.

Hand in hand, they were almost on him before Danielle spotted him. "Joey! How did you find me?"

"You're not hard to track," he said.

"What do you want?"

"I just wanted to talk to you." He wobbled a little when he stood up. He'd been drinking, but Danielle didn't seem to notice.

"Okay. About what?"

"Can we go inside?"

She glanced at Samuel. He nodded. He'd rather get this over with now while he was here with her. He wasn't concerned about their safety. One swing and he could take Joey down.

He waited while Danielle unlocked the door, and Joey followed her inside. Samuel hung back behind him, so he could make sure Joey didn't touch her.

"Come in," She looked uncomfortably at Samuel. She

mouthed "I'm sorry," behind Joey's back. He shook his head. "It's okay."

"Nice place you have here." Joey walked into her living room. Looked around.

"What do you want to talk about?" She stood with her hands on her hips, and Samuel moved to stand next to her.

Samuel knew the moment Joey saw the book on the coffee table.

"What's this?" He reached down and picked up the baby name book. He flipped through it, seeing the highlighted names and handwritten notes they had made.

He took a step toward Danielle. "It hasn't been that long. Are you?"

"Yes, Joey. I'm pregnant."

"Whose is it?" He glared at Samuel.

Samuel stood his ground. He had no idea how this would go. Maybe letting him come inside wasn't the best idea after all.

"Whose do you think it is?" Danielle quipped.

"How would I know?"

"You're the one who slept around."

"So, it's mine?" He was glaring at Danielle now.

"You're the father," she said.

"When were you planning on telling me?"

"I'm not sure I was."

"I have a right to know."

"You relinquished your rights the next day."

"I told you that didn't mean anything."

She scoffed. "Funny how you guys always say that."

He dropped the book on the coffee table. "Are you gonna keep it?"

She glared back at him.

He glanced down at the book. "Guess so since you're naming it."

"I thought you were a decent guy, Joey. We were together

for a long time. I followed you here, to be with you. But that isn't what happened, so I don't want to see you again."

"So you're gonna have this baby by yourself?"

Samuel stepped up to stand one step in front of her. "Not by herself."

Joey smiled sarcastically. "Nice going, Danielle."

She took Samuel's arm. "It's not your business. Why did you even come here?"

He shrugged. "Good question. Like you said, we were together a long time. I just wanted to make sure you were okay."

She scoffed.

"She's great," Samuel said. "As you can see. Why don't I walk you to the door?"

Joey shook his head. "Sure. Why not?"

Samuel followed Joey to the door. It was time to settle this thing once and for all.

41

---

*D*anielle sat on the sofa and realized she was trembling. It had been a mistake letting Joey come inside. Never again. Besides, he had ruined a perfectly good evening.

She heard them talking at the door, but couldn't make out their words. Maybe it was wrong to let them talk. But she was suddenly exhausted, too drained to care. After the rush of shopping and getting ready for her date with Samuel, then the adrenalin of the date itself, followed by the confrontation with Joey, she couldn't take any more.

She kicked off her shoes and curled up on the sofa. She wrapped her arms around the teddy bear and laid her head on one of the throw pillows.

WHEN SHE WOKE, SHE OPENED HER EYES TO DARKNESS. IT TOOK A second for her figure out that she was in her bed, under the covers. She was wearing nothing but her underwear and a t-shirt.

Alarmed, she sat up.

"Hi," Samuel said. He sat next to her on the bed, still wearing his tux. "How do you feel?"

"I don't know. What happened?"

He tucked a strand of hair behind her ear. "You fell asleep."

"My clothes?"

"The dress was too pretty to sleep in. I hope you don't mind terribly. I promise I was good."

She didn't mind. Though she couldn't fathom how he'd managed to undress her while she slept. "What time is it?"

"About midnight."

"So much for our last night together."

"Danielle," he said, pulling her to him. "It's not our last night together. We're going to have lots of nights together. Just not for a while, until we get things figured out."

She nestled her head beneath his chin and put her fingers in his hair. Maybe he really would come back and spend time with her. Joey had taught her a lesson. Never follow the guy. That wasn't something she was likely to forget. "What happened with Joey?"

"He won't be coming back."

"How do you know?"

"We had a man-to-man talk." Samuel rubbed his knuckles.

Danielle gasped. "You hit him?"

"Maybe just a little. Mostly, I just told him how it was gonna go, man-to-man."

She chuckled. "And what exactly does a man-to-man talk entail?"

"Sometimes fighting." She shifted, but it was too dark to see if he had bruises.

"Fortunately, this time fighting wasn't required."

"But you hit him."

"We just punched each other on the arm for good measure."

"Oh. My." She sighed.

He laughed. "Are you worried about me or him?"

"You," she murmured against his chest. "Only you."

"Good. Because all I want is for you to be happy."

"I am happy. Samuel?"

He rubbed her back. "What is it, love?"

"Will you really be back?"

"Danielle. I don't think you understand." He shifted to gently take her chin in his hands. "I'm so in love with you, I can't see straight. This baby you're carrying... I feel like it's my baby, too."

Danielle's lips curved into a smile, and her heart swelled. She put her arms around him and held him close. "I love you, too, Samuel Johnson."

"So, will you wait for me? Will you be my girl and put up with me being gone until we figure out how to be together?"

"Yes," she whispered. How was it possible that she'd fallen so deeply in love so quickly? Her grandmother had told her once that love was like that. Sometimes people grew to love each other over time, but other times, it was a sudden, unexpected meeting of the hearts.

If you ever have that happen, don't let it go. And don't let anyone stand in your way. Not even your family.

Danielle wasn't sure what her grandmother had meant about family. Her family was supportive, but she supposed she was one of the lucky ones.

42

The following Wednesday morning, Danielle sat working at her desk. She hated to do it, but she sat looking through stock photo images. After the experience of working with Avery and Jacob, she didn't feel like dealing with exclusive models at the moment.

When her phone rang with Samuel's ringtone, all thoughts went out of her head.

"Hi love," he said when she answered.

"Hi." She melted when he called her that – every time. This was the first time he'd called her in the morning since he'd left. Since he was flying during the day, they spent hours talking in the evenings.

"Do you want to have lunch?"

Her breath hitched. "Of course I do, but you're just teasing me."

"Nope, I'm serious."

"Okay." She glanced down at her casual pants and t-shirt. Did she have time to change?

"There's a catch though. I need a huge favor."

She laughed. "You want me to fly to Dallas?"

He chuckled. "Any time you want to, but not this time. This time, I'm coming there."

She smiled into the phone, but kept her voice calm. "Alright."

"They need to see my birth certificate up here for something. Insurance, I think. My mom had to go to work, but she put it in an envelope and taped it to her back door. If I send you the address, can you go get it, then meet me at the airport? I was thinking it would be a good excuse to see you."

She bit her lip. "Sure." She checked the time. It was only nine o'clock, so she had plenty of time. Even time to get home, change clothes, and maybe stop by the Dry Bar to get her hair styled.

They set up the details, and she shut down her computer. She was thankful she had a job that was based on commission, leaving her free to come and go.

While the taxi driver waited, she changed into some jeans and a new green sweater to match her eyes. She threw some makeup in a bag and rushed back to the taxi. Since Samuel had been driving her around, she'd gotten in the habit of using taxis instead of Ubers. He had given her about twenty reasons why she should stick to taxis.

After she had her hair washed and blow dried, she went into their restroom and took extra care with her makeup. She was so excited about this unexpected visit from Samuel that her hands were shaking as she applied mascara.

It was such a wonderful surprise. She'd resigned herself to a boring, lonely week, and Friday couldn't get here soon enough. Maybe this long-distance thing could work. Sure, he was coming to pick something up, but still, he was coming. She didn't have to wait all week to see him again.

She called another taxi and gave him the address Samuel had texted her. Today was one day she was second-thinking her no-driving thing. Maybe she would have to look into getting a car. Especially with a baby coming. She was going to need a car seat and who knew what else. Yes, she was definitely going to start looking for a car after the new year.

She asked the driver to wait while she got out at Samuel's house. It was a new two-story modern house with a well-manicured lawn. She went around back and stopped to study the pool and the little house on the other side of it where Samuel lived. If the taxi driver hadn't been waiting for her, she would have peeked through one of his windows. Not in a creepy way, just to catch a glimpse of the way the man she couldn't stop thinking about lived.

She would be meeting his family in four days. Just four days. In the meantime, she could focus on being productive. It certainly wouldn't hurt her career to have her weeks free to do nothing but work. She'd take a lunch to work and stay at her desk all day. Immersed in her work, maybe she wouldn't miss him quite so much.

anielle sat in the back seat of the taxi, Samuel's birth certificate tucked safely in her handbag as they approached George Bush Intercontinental Airport. The driver took her around to the Signature Flight Support building. She was familiar with this type of private area. Unlike commercial flights, she would be allowed to wait for him in the lobby.

She'd loved airports since she was a kid, probably because her father loved airports and airplanes and anything related to flying. His exuberance had been contagious and had become a part of her as well.

Still, she had butterflies in her stomach. It had been five days since she'd seen Samuel, though they'd talked on the phone daily. He would only stay long enough for them to eat lunch, then he'd be on his way back to Fort Worth.

After arriving at her building, she paid the driver and entered the lobby. It smelled like fresh-baked cookies and popcorn. She smiled at the nostalgia associated with private lobbies over the years from flying with her dad.

She was early, so his plane wasn't there yet. She took a seat where she could watch the incoming planes.

She thought of Samuel now as her boyfriend, though it was going against her rule about not dating pilots. She supposed that since she'd made the rule, she could break it.

Her father and Savannah made it work. Surely she and Samuel could also. How many men would be willing to raise another man's baby?

She shook her head. She was getting ahead of herself. He'd offered to help her out, he certainly hadn't committed to raising the baby as his own.

She recognized the plane coming in from pictures he'd shown her before it even landed. The single black stripe down the tail distinguished it from the others. She stood up and leaned against the window to be able to see him the minute he stepped from the plane.

The sky was a beautiful clear blue dome today; a perfect day for flying. He'd promised to take her up this weekend, probably Saturday, since they were having lunch with his family on Sunday. She reached inside her handbag and pulled out the envelope with his birth certificate.

She grinned as he stepped from the plane. He was wearing black pants and a white oxford shirt, the uniform her father insisted on. It was the first time she'd seen him in uniform, and her heart skipped erratically.

After he stepped from the plane, he turned and helped an attractive woman with long wavy brunette hair, looking to be about their age, step from the plane. The woman had on shades, heels, and wore a red trench coat over a short skirt. Once the two of them were on the ground, she took his hand, and they faced each other. They were too far away, but it looked like they were talking. She couldn't see Samuel's face, but the girl looked serious, then smiled.

Then they hugged. A long hug. Danielle held her breath, but even when she had to breathe, they still hugged for a few more seconds.

And then the girl stretched up and kissed him. Danielle couldn't tell if she kissed him on the cheek or the lips. As they turned and walked toward the limo that had pulled up, she slipped her hand around his elbow, their heads bent close in conversation. She kissed him on the cheek before he relinquished her to the care of the limo driver. He watched as the car drove off.

Stunned, Danielle watched as he walked back to the plane to speak to one of the line crew before approaching the lobby. She was trembling, and her thoughts were completely incoherent.

Her ears ringing, she sat on the nearest chair. She stared at the door he would be coming through shortly.

Samuel came through the lobby door a couple minutes later and quickly spotted her. A wide smile on his face, he strode toward her.

She sat, frozen, watching him walk toward her.

He stopped in front of her, and his smile disappeared. "What's wrong?" He held out a hand to help her up.

She flinched away. "No," she breathed.

"Danielle, what is it?"

"No." She stood up, threw the envelope at his feet, and practically ran toward the exit. The tears were blinding her.

"Danielle. Wait." He followed, quickly catching up with her.

He grabbed her arm. She could barely see him through the tears. She jerked away. "Leave me alone." She turned and hurried down the hallway, ignoring the people who stopped to stare at her.

When she was outside, she stood pressed against the wall until she could catch her breath. She'd been wrong about him.

He was no different from the others. No different from Joey. No different from Richard, who'd broken her heart when she was in high school. No different from other pilots who had relationships with flight attendants and passengers. She'd been so gullible. So desperate to be loved, that she'd believed him.

She had believed that he was different.

But he was like all the rest.

44

*A*nnabelle Lawson had a crush on Samuel since she was twelve years old. She was sixteen now, but Samuel would bet his life that she could get into any club with absolutely no problem. Her grandfather, Nathaniel Shannon, had doted on her – a hundred times over the level of doting on his daughter, so it was off the charts. Nathaniel lived in Houston, where he made millions running a company called Steri-Waste – medical waste removal and recycling. His daughter married a man who ran a big oil company in Dallas, so Nathaniel bought a couple of airplanes that he didn't know how to fly.

He'd gone to Louisiana Tech University and asked the flight director if he knew any recent graduates who could fly him around. Samuel's chief flight instructor had automatically called Samuel, who'd jumped at the opportunity. He'd logged countless hours flying both Nathaniel and Annabelle back and forth between Houston and Dallas. Nathaniel had preferred flying over driving, so he had kept Samuel busy, and he paid well. Samuel had saved his money, and now, at age twenty-five, he'd bought his first airplane.

As Nathaniel's flight schedule slowed and Annabelle got caught up in high school cheerleading... and boys, Samuel began looking around for other options. He was in no hurry, and didn't want to leave Houston, but when a job with Noah Worthington opened up, he had no choice but to take it. In Samuel's opinion, it was even better than getting on with a major airline.

But now Nathaniel was dying. Annabelle had called him in tears asking for a flight to Houston. The timing couldn't have been better. He'd done what he could to distract her, but she was devastated. He'd given her his sunshades to cover her swollen eyes.

He'd probably never see Annabelle again until she booked with Skye Travels some day when she was grown up. Even if then, it would be a long time. She was planning to go to university in Europe.

He watched as Danielle took the first taxi away from the airport. Had she seen him hug Annabelle? Was that what this was all about? If so, it was just a misunderstanding. He needed to follow. Would she go home or to the office? Didn't matter. He'd find her.

His phone chimed.

Damn. It was Noah. He needed him back ASAP.

anielle sat in the back of the taxi and stared out the window. She watched the traffic and the buildings of downtown approaching. She wiped her cheeks and batted back the tears that threatened to spill out.

She just needed to get home to her apartment and close out the world.

She'd had nothing good happen since she'd moved here. She'd gotten pregnant with the cheating boyfriend that she'd moved here to be with. She fallen in love with a pilot who'd moved away and now had cheated on her as well.

She'd spent enough years in therapy that she should know how to handle any crisis.

The words of her therapist came back to her with absolute clarity. *If your life isn't going the way you want it to, do something different. Think back to when things were good and try to recreate some of the good things that were working for you.*

Los Angeles. When she was in L.A. living with her mother, her life was good. She made better decisions.

She didn't fall in love in a matter of days. She dated and moved on. Or took her time with a long-term boyfriend. The fact that he eventually cheated didn't factor into her equation. He cheated in Houston, not L.A.

There was nothing here for her in Houston. She had no real reason to be here.

That was the answer. She would go home.

She laid her head back against the seat and concentrated on the things she needed to do to move. She would have to get out of her lease. But she was pregnant. That shouldn't be a problem. Extenuating circumstances.

She would quit her job. Either quit or she could work from L.A. Besides one meeting a week, she never saw anyone else at the company anyway. She could work better from the study next to her bedroom. It was much more conducive to creativity than the sterile office environment where she worked now.

Why hadn't she considered that before? She'd been grieving the loss of Joey, then Samuel had come into her life and clouded her thoughts.

She would have her mother and Grayson to help with her baby.

A smile fluttered about the corner of her lips as she realized that she and her mother could raise their babies together. They would be like siblings.

Stranger things had happened.

She let herself into her apartment. She would gather up her personal items, pack a suitcase, and call a moving company to ship everything else she needed back to L.A. The apartment had come furnished, so she didn't have furniture or appliances to deal with. The apartment had been easy to move into and would be easy to move out of.

Without looking back, she turned and walked to the apartment office. Thirty minutes later, she was free. She had until the end of the month to get out.

She could be out by this time tomorrow.

She got on the phone and arranged the moving company

and set up a flight out for tomorrow afternoon. It would have been so very much easier to just call her father and have him come get her.

But she wasn't ready to tell him.

She felt like her life was a total wreck, and she didn't want him to know just yet how bad things were going for her.

Tomorrow morning, she would go to work and talk to her boss about either quitting or working from L.A. All she had to do was to tell them she was pregnant. Everyone so far had reacted in such a cooperative way. Pregnancy was like a golden ticket to getting whatever she needed.

She hauled one suitcase onto the bed and began packing her clothes. After a few minutes, she rolled out her large suitcase. Just about everything she owned was going to fit in these two suitcases.

Her phone rang while she was in her closet gathering up shoes. She recognized the ring tone. It was Samuel. She didn't answer.

A few minutes later, her phone indicated that he'd left a message. He rarely left messages. He said he always managed to bungle them up.

As she pulled underwear from the dresser, she got a text. She ignored that, too.

She had nothing to say to Samuel Johnson and didn't want to hear anything he had to say.

She was done. She was going to take herself and her baby out of here.

By sundown, she had two suitcases standing by her front door and yellow sticky notes on everything she wanted to have shipped. Her Apple TV, a painting she'd brought with her, and a few other things.

She pulled out a trash bag and emptied the refrigerator. As she dragged it out to the trash bin at the curb, her phone rang again.

She went back inside and looked around. Everything was done.

She took a glass of orange juice from the refrigerator, one of the few things left, and went to sit on her sofa next to the teddy bear Samuel had made for her - Pappa. With his little flight suit and goggles, wearing a little stuffed camera around his neck.

What she wouldn't give for glass of wine right now.

She put her feet on the sofa and picked up the baby name book she and Samuel had spent so much time highlighting and laughing about. There were times she'd forgotten, and it had felt like it was their baby she was carrying.

She was exhausted. She remembered how he'd cooked for her while she rested. But Samuel wasn't there to make dinner. Or rub her feet.

Those days were over. Yet she was surrounded by reminders of him.

With the baby name book in her lap, she unlocked her phone and played back her messages.

46

*A*s Samuel taxied down the runway at Dallas Fort Worth Airport, he checked his phone. His only message was from Noah.

Nothing from Danielle.

He called her number, but she didn't answer.

"Danielle, it's me. I really need to talk to you. Please call me back." He paused. He hated leaving messages. Once something was said, it couldn't be taken back. "I'm confused about what happened. Noah called me back to Dallas. I didn't know what to do, so I'm back here to see what he needs. But anyway I'll call back as soon as I know. I hope you're okay."

Irritated now that he hadn't been able to follow Danielle, he went into Noah's office with a scowl on his face.

"Where have you been?" Noah asked.

"I just flew to Houston to pick up my birth certificate."

"Oh. Ok." Noah frowned at him. "And?"

"And I had plans to eat lunch with Danielle when you called me back." He left out the part about where she had run away from him in tears for some reason he could only guess about. Yet, the more he thought about it and replayed the whole thing in his mind, the more he realized that she must have misconstrued his interactions with Annabelle. He had to fix this. He had to make this right.

Noah relaxed. "It's okay. She's used to the pilot's schedule."

Exactly. Noah missed the whole point. The pilot's schedule was the major thing she didn't like about him. That and his hug with Annabelle.

"You have something on your cheek." Noah pointed out.

Samuel rubbed his cheek and came away with red lipstick on his fingertips. He groaned. He'd forgotten that Annabelle had kissed him.

This was not good. He had to fix this.

"I think she's upset. I need to go to her. To fix this."

"Does this have anything to do with a girl named Annabelle?"

Samuel blinked and had nothing to say. "I saw the flight logs. You can have tomorrow off to fix it."

"Thank you, sir." And that was exactly why Noah had endeared himself to the pilots who worked for him. "What did you need?"

"I need you to take a client to Phoenix."

"Now?"

Noah smiled. "Welcome to my world. You'll be back late."

47

Danielle sat holding her phone with her face in the teddy bear's fur. She was crying so hard that she could barely breathe. The person she needed the most wasn't there.

He'd apologized, though he said he didn't know what it was he had done. She hadn't answered. Not a single text or phone call.

Though she had his phone number halfway memorized, she blocked his number from her phone and deleted his contact information.

It was the only way she could deal with it. She had to rip the Band-Aid off quickly. She'd learned a long time ago that dragging out a break up was not the way to go. It caused too much heartache. This way, she never had to see or hear from him again.

He'd sounded tired in the last message she'd gotten only a few minutes ago. He said the girl was the granddaughter of an old friend. He said he'd given her a ride to see her dying grandfather.

Maybe he was telling the truth. Maybe he'd only been

comforting an old friend. But she saw what she saw. She couldn't unsee it. Now, whenever she saw him, she'd have that image in her head. That image of him embracing another girl.

But she wasn't that vulnerable girl she'd been at seventeen when she'd had no coping skills; when she'd felt that life wasn't worth living without her boyfriend.

The tears started again. She couldn't go through the whole thing all over again. What Joey had done had drained her and left her emotionally fragile. It probably didn't help that her hormones were all out of whack from the pregnancy.

A baby. She had a baby to take care of. That's all that mattered right now.

She would go home. She would go back to where she felt safe.

And her first appointment when she got back would be to her psychologist's office.

She needed to get over Samuel Johnson and get on with her life.

She set the teddy bear aside.

48

I t wasn't until he was flying back from Phoenix, in the dark, by radar, that Samuel realized Noah must have put it together that he was seeing Danielle. Noah had asked him to look after his daughter. And he wasn't dumb. Nonetheless, Samuel had kept Danielle's wish and hadn't said anything to her father.

He had gotten back to Dallas after Midnight, then driven the short distance to his rented apartment and fallen into bed. He had tomorrow off to see Danielle, so he didn't set a clock.

Big mistake. He didn't wake up until nine o'clock.

There was no way he would be there to take Danielle to lunch. He sat on the edge of the bed in his pajama bottoms and dialed her number again. No answer.

He jumped in the shower and threw on some jeans and a sweater. The sooner he got there, the sooner he could straighten this thing out.

He usually found being in the air calming, but not today. He couldn't shake the unease. He'd hated seeing the pain on her face and it was ten times worse knowing he'd somehow caused it.

After he landed, he grabbed the car he'd requested to be waiting for him. He assumed she would be at work, so he went to her workplace first. Her computer was turned off and had a yellow post-it note on it. Danielle wasn't in her office. He walked around her office space and knew she wasn't there and she wasn't coming back. Her space felt... different.

He wandered down the halls looking for someone to ask about her. He found two open doors. Both women shrugged and shook their heads. "People come and go all the time," one of them told him.

Her boss was out, so there was one else to ask. He needed to get to her apartment.

He rode down the elevator and dashed to her place. The apartment door stood open. Never a good sign. Was she hurt? Is that why she didn't answer? His irritation turned into true gut-wrenching concern. She could be here hurt or dying and no one would know. Except maybe the two guys taking a picture off her wall.

"What are you doing?" He stood in front of the man holding Danielle's art work. It was one of the few furnishings left that didn't have a yellow sticker on it.

The worker shrugged.

"Where is Danielle?" The pit of his stomach dropped out as it occurred to him that they may have already taken her body out.

One of the two workers took pity on him. "She moved away, man. We're gonna be right behind her, except we're driving."

"Where did she go?"

His new friend looked at the other guy who shrugged. "I don't know about her, but we're going to L.A."

Samuel dropped to the sofa that obviously didn't belong to Danielle since it didn't have a sticker on it. He allowed this information to sink in. That's when he noticed the teddy bear left on the sofa. She had left Pappa! And Pappa wasn't wearing a yellow sticker. He picked it up and ran a hand along the fur on its head. The fur was damp.

It was like a stab in his heart that she left Pappa. Samuel couldn't leave him here. He was glad he'd come here and found the little teddy bear.

Gathering up Pappa, he waved to the movers and headed out the door.

49

*D*anielle sat in the back of the taxi, riding from LAX to her house - her mother's house. She hadn't called her mother. She was just going to show up. She smiled to herself.

I am my father's child.

Her father rarely called before showing up. Both her mom and stepmother had tried to break him of that habit. His new wife had come closest.

The driver stopped in front of her house and took her two suitcases from the trunk. After he set them on the curb, Danielle paid him and the driver drove off.

Danielle stood on the curb between her two suitcases, with a tote bag on her shoulder. She watched as the taxi turned the corner and drove off. She then turned and faced her mother's house.

It was Thursday afternoon, so no one was home. She was about to upset their evening. She grabbed a suitcase with each hand and dragged them to the front. She went to the door, keyed in the code, and let herself inside.

And was met by her cat, Charlie. She picked up the cat,

squeezed him to her, and carried him with her into the living room. She needed to bring her suitcases inside, but decided she was too tired to drag them up the front porch steps. She grabbed a throw, and curled up on the sofa. She was exhausted from the trip. Exhausted from crying about Samuel. She buried her face in the cat's fur and was soothed by its purring.

She was sad that she'd left Pappa in her old apartment. It had been done in a brief moment of anger. She grabbed her phone off the coffee table and dialed the apartment complex phone number.

It took her ten minutes to convince the girl to send someone to her apartment to look for the stuffed bear. It took another thirty minutes for them call her back. The movers had already come and gone.

And there was no sign of Pappa.

When Danielle woke up, her mother was sitting on the coffee table watching her. She rubbed at her eyes and sat up. Someone had brought in her luggage. "Mom. I must have fallen asleep."

Claire nodded. "It's almost six o'clock."

Danielle hugged a throw pillow and avoided her mother's intense gaze. "I should have called."

"I guess you came by that honestly." Claire said softly.

Danielle blinked back the tears, but felt her chin trembling. Then her mother was sitting next to her, and Danielle buried her face against her mother's shoulder and cried until her tears were spent.

"Now Danielle Worthington." Claire put her hands on either side of Danielle's face and forced her to look at her. "Tell me what's going on with you."

"Everything is falling apart." Danielle's chin trembled.

"Whatever it is, I'm sure we can fix it." Claire released her.

Danielle shook her head. "I don't think so, Mom."

"You're too upset for this to be about work." Claire tilted

her head. "I know you broke up with that Joey, thank God, but you said you had a new boyfriend."

"It's so complicated. I don't know where to start."

"Start at the beginning."

Danielle's breath hitched. "I'm pregnant."

Claire sat up straight. That was her only reaction. *Years of etiquette classes.* "You're pregnant?"

Danielle sniffled. "But that's not the worst part."

"Worse than being pregnant?"

It all came out in a rush. "The worse part isn't being pregnant. It's because the father is Joey. And because I love Samuel. He would have been a great dad, but he found someone else."

Her mother scowled at her. "It might take a little time to sort all this out."

Danielle almost smiled. She'd made the right decision to come home.

50

*S*amuel sat between his two grandmothers at Pappa's Burgers and stared at his food. He ordered fried catfish – something he'd never ordered here before. He'd eaten a few bites and moved his food around on his plate.

It was Sunday dinner with the family. The day Danielle was supposed to meet his family. Samuel had been a ghost of man since he'd walked out of her deserted apartment.

He'd never known anyone to be so determined to break up that they'd moved across the country the next day. In all fairness, though, he understood her wanting to be with her mother.

But he just needed her to listen. To understand that he hadn't done anything wrong. He'd been so excited to see her. And then she'd run off – across the country.

"What's gotten into you, dearie?" His grandmother Veronica asked.

He shook his head and straightened in his chair. "It's nothing." He attempted to smile.

"You were supposed to bring your girl today."

Everyone knew of course, but Veronica was the first person to bring it up. "She's not talking to me right now."

"Nonsense. Why wouldn't a girl want to talk to a handsome young man like yourself?"

"It was a misunderstanding, but she's made her decision. She doesn't date pilots."

"Samuel Johnson." He turned to face his grandmother. His affable grandmother looked rather stern at the moment. "I know it hurt when Jessica was taken from you."

Samuel looked away. It had crushed him to lose Jessica, but since he'd met Danielle, she'd become a memory to him. He was ashamed to admit it.

Maybe his grandmother was the one person he could talk to about Danielle.

"Grandma. There's something about her I was wondering if I could talk to you about."

"You can talk to me about anything."

"She says she doesn't date pilots." His moment of resolve crumbled at the last minute.

"Nonsense. She'll get over that. What is it you really wanted to ask me about?"

Samuel chuckled. "When I met her, she was expecting a child with her ex-boyfriend." He kept his eyes down. Now, at least, his grandmother would stop asking about her, and he would start finding him someone *respectable* to date.

When his grandmother didn't respond, he looked up at her.

She shook her head. "Samuel. Is that why you let her go?"

"I didn't…" He looked away from his grandmother's piercing gaze. "She left me."

His grandmother patted his arm. "How do you feel about her being pregnant?"

"I wish the baby was mine." Samuel blurted.

"Why did she leave?"

"She saw me with a client. A young girl. And she must have

misinterpreted. She… the girl hugged me. Maybe Danielle thought I was cheating on her."

"Were you?"

"No. Of course not. I love—" He looked at his grandmother. "her." It was first time he'd said it out loud. *I should have told her.*

His grandmother grinned. "Listen to me," Veronica said. "If you want this girl, then you have to do whatever it takes."

"I don't think there's anything I can do. She won't answer my calls, and she moved to California."

"Well, that is a bit of an obstacle." Grandma Veronica took a swallow of sweet tea. "But if a man wants the girl…"

He turned and looked into her eyes. "If you want this girl, then you've got to find a way to win her back. This is not the same as what happened to Jessica. You have a chance to turn this girl around. She may say no, but you surely have to do anything and everything to get her back."

"But—"

She held up a finger. "No buts, Samuel. It's time for you to take control of your life."

51

*D*anielle was home alone when she got the flowers. And the letter.

Her eyes widened when she opened the door to the delivery guy holding the vase of three red roses.

Then she caught herself. They would be for her mother, of course, from Grayson. He was always doing little things to surprise her.

"I have a delivery for Danielle Worthington." The delivery boy said, holding the vase toward her.

"Me?" She took the flowers, but kept them at arm's reach.

"Are you Danielle?"

"Yes."

"The guy asked me to give you this letter, too."

Danielle took the envelope, too, and glanced past him, but didn't see anyone watching. "Who?"

"I don't know. Some guy who came into the flower shop. I think there's a card."

"Okay." Danielle took the flowers and closed the door, the delivery boy forgotten. Her mind whirled. Whoever had sent her flowers had bought them in person. Who would be in L.A.

to personally buy flowers to send her when they could have brought them?

Her mind darted to Samuel, but surely if he was here and knew where to find her, he'd come by. *He doesn't know how I would react.*

She took the flowers to the coffee table and opened the card. Someone had scrawled *Best Wishes* on it. Not helpful at all.

She opened the sealed envelope.

Dear Danielle,

I hope you're doing well. I'm sorry I wasn't the boyfriend you were looking for. I'm just not ready to settle down. I hope you're happy with your new boyfriend. He seemed like a nice guy, even though he did give me a black eye when I told him I didn't even know if I was the father.

Danielle rubbed her forehead. Samuel had managed to leave that part out.

I know I'm the father. You're a good girl. You deserve to be happy. So I'm not going to bother you. I'm going to leave you to raise our child as you see fit. If there ever comes a time when you need me for anything, you know how to get in touch with my mother. I told her about you and the baby. She wasn't happy about my choice, but she agreed to contact me.

Joey

. . .

P.S. IF YOU WANT CHILD SUPPORT, JUST LET MY MOTHER KNOW, AND I'll take care of it.

SHE READ THE LETTER A SECOND TIME. THE ONLY REALLY NEW information was that Samuel had given him a black eye. She wasn't quite sure what to think about that. Samuel did not seem like the kind of guy who would hit someone.

The fact that he had hit someone in defense of her honor sent a flurry of emotions through her that she couldn't even begin to sort out.

And what had prompted Joey to send this letter to her? He could easily have just let the whole issue alone. A touch of conscience perhaps? They had known each other a long time after all.

Nonetheless, it was a relief that he wasn't planning to seek custody of their child – her child. And she didn't need or want his money. That wasn't even an issue.

She was on her own. Thoughts of Samuel swirled in her mind. She had thought he would be there for her. But she had chosen to block him out of her life. She wanted someone whom she could trust with all her heart.

52

One Month Later

S amuel stood next to Noah Worthington at the window overlooking the tarmac at Dallas Love Field Airport. They both wore black pants, white oxford shirts, and black hats with silver braiding, the uniforms of Skye Travels.

"I should probably call Savannah or Danielle to let them know we're running late." Noah said, but made no move to do so.

"Yeah," Samuel kept his gaze on the storm gathering in the west. He swallowed the lump in his throat at hearing Danielle's name.

"It's okay," Noah held his iPad toward Samuel. "We can still make it."

Samuel looked at the radar showing the storm. He closed his eyes and squeezed the bridge of his nose.

He tried to ignore the pain in his heart. There was nothing he could do about it at the moment.

"See that break in the storm – here," Noah held a finger

over a clear area on the radar. "We can take off and get above the clouds."

Samuel opened his eyes and blinked. *Focus.* He pointed to the image near Birmingham. "You know they won't approve it. And even if they did, look at this area. We'll never be able to land."

Noah checked his watch. "I can't call Savannah."

"Why not?" Samuel asked, but his thoughts were already back on Danielle. Danielle was with Savannah right now. They were getting ready for Savannah's graduation from Auburn University with a Ph.D. in psychology.

"I don't want her to know I screwed up," Noah wore a miserable expression. "I can't let her down."

Well, hell. Samuel was still confused about why Noah had brought him on this flight. Noah had to remember that he and Danielle were no longer together. Samuel hadn't tried to contact Danielle after he found Pappa in her deserted apartment. The message was too loud and clear.

Even though it went against his better judgment, the least he could do was to go along with Noah. He understood Noah's need to be there for his wife.

He followed Noah out onto the tarmac and boarded Noah's Cessna with the name Skye Travels emblazoned in red across the fuselage.

He sat in the copilot's seat and watched patiently as Noah checked the radar again and called in to the Airport Traffic Advisory System and listened to the recording.

This was Samuel's first time to fly with Noah. By reputation, Noah was one of the best pilots. As far as Samuel could tell, Noah was about to make a decision based on emotion instead of good judgment. He bit his tongue as Noah radioed in to the control tower requesting permission to take off.

Samuel put on his own headset so he could listen in. "We're

not going," he said after the negative confirmation came through.

Noah turned in his seat and looked pointedly at Samuel. "We will go."

Samuel shrugged and sat back in his seat to prepare for a long wait.

After about ten minutes of silence from Noah, the rain began to slow, and it looked like the storms were moving away.

Noah sent in an emergency request to take off.

Samuel closed his eyes and tried not to think about Danielle. He tried not to wonder what she was doing right now. Three months pregnant. She would be starting to show a bit now. A baby bump. Danielle was adorable. He imagined that now that the nausea had subsided, she was already getting that glow that only expectant mothers got. They would say it was too early for her to be glowing, but Samuel had seen it. He saw it in the glint of her eyes when she smiled at him.

When she hadn't thought he was watching her work on a design.

"Go ahead, Skye Flight 23. Ready for take-off Runway 31 right," the controller said in his headset, knocking Samuel out of his reverie. "No way." He straightened in his seat.

Noah grinned as he flipped switches bringing the aircraft to life. "You have to have faith," he said.

"Determination is more like it."

"Semantics." Noah guided the plane down toward the runway. "Let's go see our girls."

Samuel kept his focus on the controls and ignored Noah's words. He would think about that later. For now, it was going to be interesting to see the famous Noah Worthington at work. All he had to do was keep his mind off anything Danielle-related.

Once they were in flight, however, there wasn't a lot of distraction to keep his thoughts in check.

Noah wanted him to go to Savannah's graduation reception with him, even knowing Danielle would be there. He had a sick feeling in his stomach when he thought about seeing Danielle. It had been about four weeks. Would she be with someone else? Probably not. Since Noah had brought him along, she must not be seeing anyone else, at least not seriously.

She would probably be showing now. How was she coping with being pregnant? He thought that by now, he'd be rubbing her feet, at least on the weekends. He knew now that anything beyond weekends would have been a challenge. He was usually up at six, flying all day, then just time for a quick happy hour before falling into bed. Only to get up and do it all over again the next day.

He'd spent the weekends at home, mostly with his family. With the holidays coming up, his mother had kept him distracted with decorating the house. But despite her efforts, it made Samuel even sadder that he didn't have Danielle to do things with.

He kept a picture they had taken together the Friday before he left. They'd had a nice dinner until her ex had shown up. Samuel hoped the guy hadn't followed her to L.A.

He wasn't opposed to tracking him down if he thought Joey was harassing her.

He had lots of other pictures of them, too, from the photo shoot. Though they hadn't started seeing each other at that point, those pictures conveyed intimacy. An intimacy that had begun growing even before they knew it was there. Looking back, Samuel was enchanted from the moment he met Danielle.

She had never returned any of his phone calls or texts. If Noah knew that she'd moved, he hadn't said anything to Samuel. In fact, they rarely talked about Danielle at all.

Samuel was trying to let her go. But being around her father, working with him, even now flying with him, left the wound open. Sometimes, he'd say something or make a facial expression that reminded him of Danielle. He thought about her all the time.

He glanced over at Noah, who was checking the radar again. Noah knew. He knew Danielle had gone back to L.A., Samuel would put money on it. There was no way his daughter moved across the country without her father knowing about it. Noah was just being respectful of Samuel's feelings by not bringing it up.

It was a little odd, though, that he sometimes acted like they were still together. Like today. *Let's go see our girls.*

One day. One day he would have the chance to talk to her again. To straighten things out between them. Probably not today, though, since today was about Savannah and family.

It was time though. Time to put this misunderstanding behind them.

*D*anielle sat on the sofa surrounded by family at Savannah's house on Lake Martin near Auburn, Alabama. Her mother, Claire with her new husband, Grayson were there. Her stepmother, Savannah, was there of course, with her baby, Aria. Danielle's grandmother, Emily, was there, too.

It was interesting that Noah's ex-wife and current wife had become friends of sort over the years. Danielle supposed that she was the link holding them together. Mother and stepmother. They were similar in many ways. Very cultured. Neither one of them would be caught yelling or slamming a door. They probably wouldn't run away from a relationship like Danielle had, either.

The only person missing from today's gathering was Noah – Savannah's new husband.

And Samuel.

Danielle hadn't known that she could miss someone quite so fiercely as she missed Samuel.

She knew that Noah and Samuel were flying in together.

What she didn't know was whether or not Samuel would be coming to the graduation party.

It didn't keep her from watching the door.

The rain was falling in torrents now. She shifted her gaze toward the windows along the back of the house and watched the storm roll in across the lake. Someone had turned on the electric fireplace. That and the lights from the Christmas tree reflected in the window. The tune *I'll be home for Christmas* played in the background.

Danielle checked the cell phone she held in her hand. Even now, after a month, she missed the frequent texts she'd become so accustomed to from Samuel.

Savannah sat on the other end of the sofa, also staring at her silent cell phone.

"No word from Noah?" Danielle asked.

"No. You?" Danielle heard the anxiety in Savannah's voice.

Danielle shook her head. *Samuel would have stayed in touch.*

"They must be in the air." Savannah was known for her optimism.

"Probably," Danielle agreed. Still, a tendril of anxiety slithered up her spine. Her father had done a one-eighty since he'd been married to Danielle's mother. He stayed in touch now. His marriage to Savannah was nothing like his marriage to Claire.

Still. Danielle maintained her conviction that once a man was away, it was far too easy to lose touch and for a relationship to fall apart. The current circumstance was a case in point. Her father had missed Savannah's graduation. Without a single word.

"Did you text Samuel?" Savannah asked.

"We broke up," Danielle responded automatically, though she knew that Savannah was well aware of this.

"Right," Savannah said.

Danielle tapped her phone. Looked back toward the window.

"Still," Savannah insisted, "he'd probably answer you. Then we'd at least know that Noah is okay."

Danielle frowned. Damn Savannah for invoking the fear and anxiety that she had learned to live with regarding her father's flying.

Noah was a good pilot. "No," Danielle said. "He's late because of the storm. He'll be here when the weather clears." She took a deep breath and reached out and touched Savannah's arm. "I'm sorry he missed your graduation. I can't imagine what a huge disappointment that must be."

"It's part of the package. I knew that going in. I trust him. I trust him with every fiber of my being."

"He'll be here." Danielle ignored Savannah's comment about trust. They weren't talking about trust. *Everyone knows.* Everyone had to know that she broke up with Samuel because she didn't trust him. Maybe Savannah thought it was unjustified.

"You're right," Savannah said. Waited a beat. "I guess it was a little strange to think about marrying someone so much like your father."

Danielle didn't want to talk about Samuel. She missed him so much it ached. The fact that he was like her father wasn't strange. One of the things she liked about Samuel was that he was like her father. It was the thing that she most liked and most feared.

She feared days like today. Days when he didn't call. Just like Noah hadn't called.

"I met him a couple of weeks ago. He seemed like a nice guy, but then… you would know him better than anyone else."

Danielle fought the urge to walk away from her stepmother. She turned away from Savannah, her chin trembling, as she considered her words.

Yes, Samuel was a nice guy. And yes, she knew him better than anyone else. She was the one who knew just how kind he was. How generous. And how much he had cared about her.

Savannah's mother, Emily, walked over, Aria on her hip. "I think we should go ahead with the cake," she said.

Savannah nodded. "Of course." And took her child from Emily.

Emily served cake and punch. Danielle ate a few bites, but barely tasted it. Savannah also barely touched her cake. Danielle's heart went out to her, despite her irritation with her stepmother's accurate observations. Savannah was in obvious pain, and it was her graduation party.

Danielle stood next to the Christmas tree, facing the front door - she couldn't help herself. Besides, it wasn't strange to be worried about her father. In fact, she was worried about both of them – her father and the man she still loved.

After Savannah tossed her plate into the trash, she picked up her daughter, who'd crawled behind her into the living room.

With the exception of the Christmas music in the background, the room was quiet. Waiting.

The doorbell rang. As far as Danielle knew, no one else had been invited to Savannah's small celebration. Noah wouldn't ring the doorbell. *It could be Samuel coming in before Noah.* Samuel would ring the doorbell.

Danielle and Savannah reached the door at the same time. Danielle realized what she was doing and stopped to stand back. It was Savannah's house.

Savannah opened the door to two men wearing black suits. That little tendril of fear was more like a full-blown fire now.

"Mrs. Worthington?" The older of the two asked.

"Yes," Savannah said, handing Aria over to Danielle. Danielle took the cooing baby and cradled her close, but her eyes were locked on the men at the door.

"We're with the FAA. You're listed as next of kin on Noah Worthington's contact record."

Savannah grabbed the edge of the door and fell to her knees. "Noah," she said, just as Danielle reached her side.

54

*A*bout thirty minutes out, Noah gave Samuel control of the plane. "There's a thunderstorm just north of Auburn Airport," he pointed out. "We'll go in from the south and land on runway 36."

They began their descent to Auburn Airport. "We're in the correct position," Samuel said, but even as he said the words, the plane shifted.

"We're in a microburst." Noah said.

"Descending…" Samuel gave the plane full power, but the descent continued.

Altitude warning alarms began beeping. "What the--? Give me the controls."

"Landing gear!" Samuel flipped a switch.

Noah pulled out of the drive with full power. "Something's wrong with the system," he muttered.

"We're gonna stall."

"I'm going to do a controlled descent."

"We're too high." Samuel held onto his seat, his knuckles white.

"I switched off," Noah said. "We'll recover out of it."

"Yes," Samuel agreed. "We're leveling off. Everything's fine now."

Noah exhaled. Gauges indicated the runway ahead. They were on path. Samuel blew out his breath. Everything was good.

"We made it." Noah engaged the thrust reversers to start slowing them down.

The plane was set in full reverse, but they were going too fast, and the end of the runway was getting close. Seeing the end of the runway was something he *never* wanted to do.

Noah hit the brakes, but the plane started sliding on the wet runway.

They checked the antiskid. Engaged.

System failure.

Something wasn't right. Noah checked the annunciator light to see if there was system failure, but it was on.

Samuel gripped the edges of his seat as they slid off toward the end of the runway. "We're gonna crash," he said through his teeth.

They were going too fast. Much too fast to stop now. They braced themselves as they went into a full skid off the runway.

The last thing that flashed through Samuel's mind was an image of Danielle smiling up at him and the feel of her lips on his.

55

They made it to East Alabama Medical Center in Opelika in record time. Grayson drove Emily's SUV with everyone else packed into the seats, Aria included. There had been no time to think. Someone, Emily and maybe Grayson, had grabbed all their handbags and ushered them out the door.

Savannah had known where to go and what to do. Everyone else just followed. Danielle was in a daze. The men from the FAA had said Noah was alive, but that they needed to get to the hospital.

They hadn't said anything about Samuel.

Noah was in surgery, so the whole family was sent to a waiting area to sit. And pace.

Her father had to be alright. Though she'd dogged Savannah's heels and listened to every conversation, no one had indicated that he was very bad off.

And no one mentioned Samuel.

Danielle paced across the waiting room floor a couple of times. Emily had gotten Aria to sleep. Savannah was on the edge of her seat. Claire sat with Grayson, their attention on his iPad.

Without a word, Danielle went out to the nurse's station. "Can you tell me where Samuel Johnson is?"

The nurse looked at her over her glasses, typed on the computer, and shook her head. "We don't have anyone by that name."

"Maybe he came in without a name. He was with Noah Worthington. In the crash."

The nurse shook her head. "The ambulance only brought in one person."

"That can't be," Danielle said, turning on her heel and running back to the waiting room.

"Savannah, are you certain Samuel was with Dad? The nurse said he isn't here." Her words came out in a rush. *What if he hadn't survived?*

Savannah's brows furrowed. "Yeah. When I talked to Noah this morning, he said they were both coming. He said Samuel was excited to see you."

"He knows we broke up."

"Well, either way, he was bringing Samuel with him to graduation and to the party."

"The ambulance only brought in one person. Where is he?"

Savannah frowned. "That airplane is rated for two pilots. There was another pilot on that plane." She was out of her chair and on her way to the nurse's station.

"Danielle," Claire called.

Danielle stopped in her plan to follow Savannah and instead went to sit next to her mother.

"Are you okay?" Claire asked, placing a hand on Danielle's arm.

Danielle shook her head, feeling the tears gathering in her eyes. "No one knows where Samuel is. He was on the plane with Noah."

Claire glanced at Grayson. "How can that be?" Her voice trailed off with an unspoken realization.

Grayson shook his head. "Not necessarily," he muttered.

Danielle stood up, took a step, and came back to stand in front of them. "I have to find him."

Savannah rushed back. "They took him to Birmingham - UAB."

"Oh no!" Danielle said. That could only mean the worst. "How is he?" She bit her lip even as she asked.

"She didn't know," Savannah said. "But they flew him straight to UAB by Lifeflight."

Danielle felt the bottom fall out of her stomach. No. No. Not Samuel. Not sweet, kind, loving Samuel. "I have to go. I have to go to him." She turned to Claire and held out her hand. "I need the car."

"Danielle, honey, we flew. We don't have our car."

Danielle put a palm on her forehead. "Right." She couldn't think straight. She needed a car.

Emily stepped forward and held out her keys. "Take mine," she said.

"Mom! How will we get home?" Savannah asked.

Emily raised her eyebrows at her daughter as Danielle took the keys from her hand. "We'll figure it out."

Keys in hand, Danielle raced from the room toward the front of the hospital. Did she even know which car belonged to Emily? It was an SUV. *I'll find it.*

She dashed out into the cold and looked around the parking lot for an SUV. Fortunately, there was only one in sight.

Getting into the driver's seat, she put her head on the steering wheel and took deep breaths. She had no idea which way to go.

"I'm the daughter of a pilot," she told herself. "I've lived in L.A. and Houston. Surely, I can drive to Atlanta."

If only I had an airplane. I could navigate myself there.

GPS.

With sudden inspiration, she used her phone to map her way to the hospital in Atlanta.

The SUV felt huge in her hands. She knew how to drive. She just didn't like to drive.

Within minutes, she was on Highway 280, and it looked like a straight shot from here.

She relaxed her hands on the wheel for the first time since she'd put the vehicle into drive.

Maybe she should have waited to see how her father came through his surgery. But surely, he was going to be okay, since they'd kept him there in Auburn. *Or maybe he was too critical to leave.*

No. Samuel's words came back to her. *Take a deep breath, Danielle. Everything is going to work out.*

Remembering how Samuel had held her hair while she threw up, her eyes teared up, and the road in front of her blurred. She blinked back the tears to be able to see better.

He'd been there for her every step of the way. He'd known she was pregnant before she was, and had taken her to the doctor.

He'd even offered to be there for her and to help raise the baby.

When Joey had shown up, her ex had left with a black eye and wounded pride.

And she'd walked away from him without even a word; without giving him a chance to redeem himself.

With the perfect man standing right in front of her, declaring his love.

She'd been afraid. Afraid of being hurt. Again.

It was stupid. Being apart from him hurt like hell.

They'd been attached at the hip from the moment they met.

Now, for nearly a month, she'd been nothing but miserable. And for what reason? He was lying in a hospital – perhaps even fighting for his life. She may never even get to see him again. To talk to him. To hold his hand. To kiss him.

What she wouldn't give to have just one more day with him. One more day to have things back the way they were before.

I was wrong. It hurts more to be without him than to be with him.

There was nothing wrong with being like her father. Noah Worthington was a good man, and Samuel didn't even have her daddy's bad quality of not staying in touch.

Samuel wasn't Noah. And he certainly wasn't Joey. Or Richard. Samuel hadn't cheated on her. In her heart, she knew that he'd been telling the truth about his passenger.

As she got into the city traffic, she forced herself to focus and not to think about Samuel, a nearly impossible task.

When her phone rang, she hit speaker. It was her mother.

"Noah is out of surgery and is doing fine."

"Thank God," Danielle said. "I have to go, Mom. I'm hitting traffic."

"Are you sure you're okay to drive? You don't even know where you're going."

Danielle laughed a humorless laugh. It sounded like something between a laugh and a croak. "It's a little late to be worried now. I'm fifteen minutes out. I'll call you when I know something."

She got off the phone and sat forward in the seat.

I have to make this right. When I see Samuel, I'll tell him.

I'll tell him I love him.

56

When Samuel woke up, he was in a helicopter with an oxygen mask over his mouth. As he lay there with his eyes closed, slowly getting his bearings, the last thing he could remember was seeing the end of the runway ahead of them. They'd crashed then.

When he opened his eyes, the medic greeted him cheerfully and removed the mask. He quizzed Samuel on the basics – his name, the date, where he was when the accident happened.

"Where are you taking me?" he asked.

"UAB."

"Where's that? I'm from Houston."

"Birmingham. One of the best hospitals in the country."

"Noah?" His held as breath as he waited for an answer. Danielle's father had to be okay.

"They took him to the local hospital. He had a broken bone. Probably doing surgery, but he'll be okay."

Samuel blew out a breath, and the medic put the oxygen back on his mouth. Noah would be okay then.

He began replaying the last moments before the crash. System failure. That's all it could have been. Noah did everything right. They would try to blame it on the weather and pilot error, but Samuel had landed in worse. The weather had nothing to do with it. Noah had accounted for the slippery runway.

"We're ten minutes out. Is there anyone we can contact for you?"

Danielle.

Danielle was always his first thought. But she'd made it clear that they were no longer a couple. That she didn't want a future with a pilot. Not in words, but in actions.

Something had gone wrong. Terribly wrong. She had been right. He could have been killed.

The irony was that he now had an automatic four months off. A pilot couldn't fly for one hundred twenty days after a concussion. It was almost perfect timing. He would have been around all the time to help her get ready for the baby. The baby that he had been ready to claim as his own.

The helicopter landed at UAB, and Samuel was carried inside on a stretcher. He'd hesitated long enough to avoid answering the medic's question about who to contact about his accident. He felt well enough. He didn't want to alarm his family. The last thing he needed was for them to come flying out here to Alabama from Houston when he was fine. He would tell them all about it at their next Sunday dinner.

Since he was about to have four months off, he could spend some long overdue time with his family.

The next couple of hours were spent with doctors and an MRI. And more doctors. They finally decided that they would keep him for observation for forty-eight hours.

After getting set up in a private room, a nurse came in with a plastic bag containing his clothes and his cell phone.

He grabbed his cell phone like a man dying of thirst would grasp a cup of water. He had only one text message. It was from his sister reminding him to be there for Sunday dinner.

Since it was in two days, he wouldn't make it this week. He'd make an excuse later.

Finally left alone, he laid his head back and closed his eyes. Maybe after a little nap, he'd call his sister. He wasn't over the breakup with Danielle and now this crash. He could use a friendly voice in his ear.

The sense of isolation – being stuck here in a hospital somewhere in Alabama – was overwhelming. To get through it, he imagined he was flying in his Mooney single-engine high above the clouds. His thoughts soon settled enough that he was able to drift off to sleep.

In what seemed like only a few minutes, he opened his eyes to a smiling blonde standing over his bed. He blinked. She wasn't wearing a uniform, and she didn't look familiar.

"I'm sorry," the girl, who looked to be college-aged, smiled. "You didn't answer when I knocked, so I came on in to see if you needed anything."

Samuel shook his head. Why would this girl, this stranger, be here to check on him?

"I'm here with the Sigma Kappa Sorority, and we're visiting people at the hospital with Alzheimer's Disease. I know you don't have it, but since you hit your head, you were kinda the closet person I could find to talk to that would count."

Samuel groaned. The girl was talking, and he couldn't quite follow what she was saying. He closed his eyes and drifted back to sleep. When he woke, Danielle was there, leaning over him. His heart soared. He held out his hand and squeezed hers. She'd come!

"I'm so happy you're here. I've missed you more than you can ever know."

anielle rushed into the ER and found her way to the desk.

"Samuel Johnson," she struggled to catch her breath.

"Your name," the clerk peered at her over narrow glasses.

"Danielle." She tried to smile. Anything to keep from grabbing the computer from the woman and looking herself.

The woman's hands remained in her lap. "We have a family-only policy for giving out information."

"I'm his fiancé," she blurted.

The woman tilted her head as she seemed to consider.

"Please," Danielle pleaded. "Just tell me if he's even here. I just drove in from Auburn. And we're from Houston." She didn't fight the tears that filled her eyes. Crying on demand was a talent that she'd never mastered... until becoming pregnant. Now, the pregnancy hormones had opened up a whole new world.

The clerk tapped on her computer keys. "He's in room 532," she said.

"Thank you," Danielle said and took off toward the elevators.

When she got off the elevator and approached his room, she stopped. What was she supposed to say? *Hi. I know I broke up with you. But I was so worried.*

Maybe it was best if she didn't say anything.

Her heart pounded in her chest as she put one foot in front of the other. Now that she was here, it took every ounce of strength to keep moving forward.

She heard female laughter as she approached his room. Probably a nurse trying to cheer him up. She put a hand on the doorknob and turned it. As the door opened, she wondered if she was supposed to knock first. Danielle had no experience with hospitals. She'd gone with her mother once to visit her grandmother, but that was it.

As the door swung open, Samuel smiled. With a two-second sweep, she took in the situation. Definitely not a nurse.

Samuel sat propped on pillows in the bed. His attention was on a young lady standing at his bedside. Definitely not a nurse. As she drew closer, she saw that he was holding the girl's hand. She took another step, though her brain was frozen. She stopped just inside the door and heard Samuel's words. "I'm so happy you're here. I've missed you more than you can ever know." It barely registered that his eyes were half closed.

The girl saw Danielle first and turned, concern and confusion shadowing her face. Samuel followed her gaze. His eyes widened in disbelief. "Danielle," he breathed. He looked back at the girl standing next to his bed, holding his hand.

Danielle felt a wave of heat setting her blood to boil. This. This was exactly why she would never marry a pilot.

"You're here." He murmured, looking back at the other girl. "How?" Then turned his gaze back to Danielle.

"I drove." Her voice was barely a whisper, but her heart was in her throat.

"Wait."

Danielle turned around and quietly walked back down the

hall. *Never make a scene,* her mother had told her a million times.

Once she was in the parking lot and inside the vehicle, she locked the door and the tears wracked her body. She cried harder than she had ever cried before. Even harder than the time she had taken her mother's Xanax with her father's alcohol.

That had been years ago, and she had never felt that way since.

Not until now. Now she felt like her world had crashed at her feet in a thousand pieces. Even as she'd broken up with Samuel, she'd clung to the belief in her heart that he was different. That he would never hurt her.

He had no idea what it had taken for her to drive to this hospital. Not only the drive itself, but to take the risk that he might want to see her.

He hadn't needed her after all. He'd moved on. Without her. Just like she'd known he would.

It will pass. Years of therapy coalesced in that moment to give her strength. She wiped away the tears and lifted her head. It was raining now. She watched the raindrops slide down the windshield and let them wash away her pain along with it.

Maybe it was the hormones, but whatever it was, it was too much. Samuel deserved better.

I need to get myself together.

Every instinct had her going back up to his room. It was a misunderstanding. She could straighten it out in a minute.

Samuel deserves someone he can make a baby with. His own baby.

I love him too much. I have to let him go.

She put on her seatbelt and put the SUV in reverse.

She needed to get Emily's car back to her. Then she needed to get back to L.A. and back to work. Authors were waiting on their covers, and she had to design them.

And more importantly, she had to get ready to bring home a baby.

58

*S*amuel had his feet on the ground before the nurse darted into the room and grabbed hold of his ankles. "Where do you think you're going?" she admonished.

"Danielle," he said, pulling away.

"You can't leave," she told him.

"I can." He made it as far as the elevator. As he stood waiting for the elevator, he knew. He knew he wasn't going to catch her.

She had been moving too fast, and he had lost precious time before he reacted. And that nurse had held him back, and now that same nurse was there grabbing one arm while an orderly took the other. "It's not a good idea for you to leave right now," The man's voice was gentle. Understanding. Unlike Nurse Ratched whose fingers were digging into his upper arm.

He allowed them to lead him back to his room – as if he had a choice. He had some things to think about anyway.

First, and most importantly, Danielle had driven here from Auburn; the other side of Auburn if he remembered correctly. For a girl who never drove, that was quite an accomplishment.

The girl from Sigma Kappa was still there when he got back

into his room. "I appreciate your kindness," he told her, "but I'd like some time to myself now."

The girl left as he climbed back into his bed and lay there with his eyes closed.

He had quite a few things to think about.

59

Two weeks later…

*D*anielle now remembered why she avoided commercial flying when at all possible. The hassle had gotten out of hand. Especially at this time of year, just days before Christmas. She sighed as the older woman sitting next to her pulled a tote bag of merrily-wrapped presents from under the seat in front of her. Yes, she should have taken her father up on that offer.

She walked through the gate at the airport in Fort Worth. Her pulse rate was a little too high. Maybe it was from flying commercial. Her father had offered to send someone to pick her up, but she'd said she needed some time alone. To think.

Fortunately, the expense of booking a flight over and back the same day was so ridiculously outrageous that she had booked a one-way ticket. She had made a good decision in counting on her father getting her back to California.

Or Samuel.

She had come to Fort Worth under the guise of visiting her

father, but in truth, she wanted to see Samuel. Maybe it was the sentiment of the holiday season, but she wanted to make things right with him. She hadn't given him a chance to explain himself either time before running away. Something nagged at the back of her brain about the two incidents. Maybe it was his bewildered expression. And that it just didn't fit with what she knew about him. Whatever it was, she wanted to see him. To talk to him.

Her father stood waiting for her just outside the door. It was one of the perks of being a pilot that he had free reign at the airport. He greeted her with a big bear hug, as always.

"I'm so glad you're okay." It was the first time she'd seen him since he was in the hospital, and she had to blink back tears.

"So am I. It's good to see you, too. No luggage?"

"Nah. I'm just here for the day."

"Alright. Let's get lunch." Together, they walked through the airport, then outside to his car. "Are you craving anything in particular?"

"Pizza." She'd run through seafood, then Mexican, now anything with cheese.

"Pizza it is." Driving away from the airport, he took them straight to a small pizzeria.

"You knew just where to go." Danielle said.

Noah looked a little sheepish. "You know pizza is my weakness. I eat here whenever I can come up with an excuse. Just don't tell Savannah."

Danielle laughed. She loved that she and her father were close enough that they had things they did. Things that neither her mom nor Noah's current wife, Savannah would need to know about. Like eating pizza.

After they ordered, while they waited on their pizza, Noah peered at his daughter. "I know you didn't fly all the way over here to eat pizza. Although I have to admit I've done it myself."

"Yeah." She looked away. There was nothing she couldn't tell her father. That didn't mean it was always an easy thing to do. "I was hoping I could see Samuel."

Noah's eyes widened. Danielle's heart tripped. Surely, if something had happened to him, someone would have told her.

"You didn't try calling him?"

"Dad. I deleted his phone number."

"Pumpkin, you probably shouldn't do things like that."

"I know. But is he here today?"

"He has a mandatory one hundred twenty days off after a concussion."

"So… is he coming back?"

Noah shrugged. "I don't know."

The only way Danielle had communicated with Samuel was through his cell phone. "Daddy, does he still have the company cell phone?"

"Yeah, but he doesn't answer it."

Danielle stared into space. There had to be a way.

"Danielle." Noah pulled her attention back to him. "What happened with him?"

"I saw him. In Houston. At the airport. With another woman."

"When?"

Their pizza arrived, giving Danielle time to think back to enough details to answer her father's question. "It was the day he had me bring him his birth certificate."

Noah gaped at her. "I remember. He came back so obviously upset, but he wouldn't tell me what was wrong. He'd just taken Annabelle to Houston to see her dying grandfather."

"Annabelle?" Danielle didn't feel so good.

"Yeah." He shrugged. "A client."

"Daddy. I think I messed up."

She told him about how she'd seen Samuel at the airport and stormed off. She also told him about seeing him with the girl at the hospital. "He'd just had a concussion. I think he might have been confused." She blinked back tears. "What should I do Daddy? What would you do?"

60

Two months later…

*D*anielle sat at her desk in her home office on the
second floor of her mother's house in Los Angeles.
She had to give her mother credit. She'd accepted Danielle's
pregnancy without a hitch, and together, they had converted a
guest room into a home office for Danielle to work. Danielle
had an enviable view of the back yard – a manicured lawn with
evergreen trees blocking the neighbors.

She was lost in the world of shape shifters. This was her
biggest author yet. And the author's release date was in just six
months. And big name authors got their books out there for
preorder early.

She glanced at the calendar next to her desk and noted the
date.

February 14.

She'd gotten through Christmas and New Year's without a
boyfriend. She could get through Valentine's Day without
one.

As though to remind her that she wasn't alone, the baby in

her abdomen kicked. A little feathery kick, but a kick nonetheless. She smiled.

"Just you and me kiddo. We'll get through this just fine."

She ducked back into her work. A couple of minutes later, a movement at the door caught her attention.

She looked up and blinked.

Samuel.

Holding a bouquet of red roses.

She sat back and stared at him, then blinked again to make sure she wasn't hallucinating.

"I have a delivery for Miss Danielle Worthington."

A smile played at the corner of her lips. "Did my father send you?"

He smiled then. "No. As a matter of fact, these are from..." He shifted the bouquet. "Let me just check the card." He looked at the attached envelope. "They're from a mister Samuel Johnson. Do you know him?"

"Hmm." Her lips curved into a slight smile. "I believe he's a pilot from Dallas."

"Oh no," he said. "That's not the same person. This is Samuel Johnson, flight instructor, of L.A."

She frowned at him. "There must be a mistake. The only one I know works for my father."

"Nope," he said. "This one lives right here in L.A. Um. Can I come in?"

"Of course," she said. "I wasn't thinking." She hit save on her computer and slid it aside. "Are those for me? Really?"

He looked wounded. "And who else would they be for?" He set them on the desk, the silver vase glittering in the sunlight streaming through the window. "They're yours if you'll have them."

"It's impolite to refuse a gift." She leaned forward and sniffed one of the perfect rose buds. "Even if it is Valentine's Day."

"Is it Valentine's Day? I wondered why there was such a long line to buy flowers today."

"Ha. Ha."

He shrugged. "It seems we have a tradition. Birthdays. Valentine's Day."

"You missed Christmas." She pointed out.

"You weren't in the office," he said.

"And neither were you." *Nor did you answer your phone even after I found your number on my cell phone statement.*

"I've been off the grid for a while."

She decided to let his statement go. She wanted to see how he planned to play this out. "So how are you feeling?" She asked. "After the crash and all."

"The doctors released me."

"Both you and my father were very lucky. They said it was system failure."

"Luck had nothing to do with it. It was all due to your father's skill and experience that we came out basically unscathed."

"If you call a concussion unscathed."

"Considering the circumstances, I do."

She studied the red rose buds for a moment. They were high quality flowers. Her mother had taught her how to discern quality. "So, really, what brings you here? I'm not expecting my father."

"Your father has nothing to do with my being here."

"How did you get away? He drives a hard bargain with his pilots."

"Right." She wouldn't tell him she'd asked her father about him and already knew that. "I have a mandatory one hundred twenty-day moratorium on flying."

"For the concussion?"

"Yes. And I also quit my job."

She scoffed. "You did not."

"I most certainly did. Ask him."

She glanced at her phone. "I'm not going to ask him."

"Cause then you'd have to believe me."

"Of course I believe you. You've never lied… to… me." She said the last words slowly, realizing that those were the words she should have said to him three months ago.

"And I never will."

She nodded. Trust. Something that he had earned, despite her reluctance to give it. "So, you're visiting." She wasn't quite sure what he was telling her.

"I think we need to talk," he said.

"Right," She stood up and gestured to the day bed across the room. It was perfect for naps, but now it seemed, it was good for entertaining. Next to the day bed was a crib with pink blankets.

Samuel stopped halfway across the room and stared at the crib with a silly grin on his face. "It's a girl," he said.

Danielle smiled as she ran a hand along the now unmistakable baby bump. "Yes. I had to know."

They sat on the day bed, and she wondered where to begin. He looked good. She'd stared at his photo enough to memorize every line on his face, but he was even more handsome in person. When he looked at her, his eyes twinkled with a light that couldn't be captured in a photo.

It seemed he already knew what he wanted to say. "When I saw you in Alabama, I knew I had to do something. Whatever it took to be with you."

His words were like a warm balm settling over her soul. "Samuel…"

"Even if you hadn't left Houston, I didn't want to live like that. I didn't want to live apart and only see you on weekends. You deserve more than that."

"Even that's more than most people have."

"Maybe so. But it isn't for us."

She knew exactly what he meant. They weren't just a romantic couple. They were best friends. They wouldn't be one of those couples who only saw each other in the evenings or weekends for dinner. They were part of each other's daily lives. Or had been until she'd disappeared on him. "I guess I knew you would find me."

"You knew I could."

"And hoped you would." Words she hadn't even admitted to herself. Until now. Seeing him here, it was even more clear how much she'd missed him.

"So," he continued. "I *did* quit my job with Skye Travels."

"You really quit?"

He nodded. "I really did."

"Wow. My father didn't say anything."

"I asked him not to. To let me tell you. And I didn't tell him until two days ago. I waited because I wasn't sure how long he could keep it from you."

She waited for him to say more. He took her hand and wove his fingers through hers. "Danielle, I've moved to L.A."

"But your home is in Houston. Your family. Houston is in your blood."

"I'll get a stronger plane."

She thought about her father and how she hated that he lived so far away – in Alabama, but he worked in Fort Worth and visited her often here in California. There were perks to being a pilot, but not an unemployed pilot.

"What will you do?"

"I'm an instructor."

"I know. You said. But I mean for a job?"

"It is a job. A job that will allow me to be home in the evenings in time to make dinner and take care of you."

She stared at their hands linked together. A flight instructor. Still a pilot. She sighed. "I think I might have mentioned that I don't date pilots."

"Danielle. Seriously? Surely we've gotten past that. Give me a chance."

How could she not? She nodded.

"Will you let me take you flying?"

She laughed. "Flying is all you pilots think about."

"True. But there are some people I'd like you to meet."

61

Samuel sat next to Danielle at Pappa's Burgers, squeezed in between his two grandmothers.

"I'm so glad we finally get to meet you," Veronica Johnson said to Danielle.

"It's nice to meet you all, too."

"You'll come back to the house with us after lunch, won't you? We'd like to spend time with you."

Danielle glanced at Samuel. He shrugged.

He wasn't having to say much today. Everyone was focused on Danielle. They were so excited he'd finally brought a girl to a family function, they practically had them married off.

"Have you set a wedding date?" His older sister asked from across the table.

Danielle had the deer-in-the-headlights reaction for only a fraction of a second. He was probably the only one who saw it. "No," she said, keeping the smile on her face. "We haven't talked about that."

He'd warned her that they would be invasive – in a loving and accepting way. He squeezed her hand. It was so very nice to have someone to share his family's intensity with.

His younger sister chimed in. "You'll get married before the baby comes?"

Samuel scowled at her. He hadn't told anyone that Danielle was pregnant. When she glanced at him, he shook his head.

He could see her thoughts whirling as she decided the best way to go with this. "There's plenty of time before July to figure everything out."

He heard his mother and father whispering from his left. "A baby?"

"Did you know about this?"

His mother beamed. "Another grandchild."

"Like you don't have enough."

His mother elbowed his father. Then when there was a lull in the conversation, she said loud enough for Danielle to hear. "Welcome to the family, dear."

Danielle flushed and squeezed Samuel's hand.

Then their food arrived, and as the server distributed their plates, the conversation moved to other things. Preschools. His brother's new job. With such a big family, there was lots to keep up with.

Danielle relaxed a little and smiled at him. "I tried to warn you," he whispered.

"And I wholeheartedly appreciate that."

He chuckled. "I guess you'll believe me next time."

"Believing and experiencing are a leap apart."

62

*D*anielle and Samuel were swept away to his grandparent's house along with the rest of the family after lunch.

"Can I show you around?" Samuel asked.

"Sure." The rest of the family settled into the living room and spilled into the kitchen. The house was full of large windows with an open floorplan. He led her around to the parlor.

"It's a pretty house," Danielle said, looking at Samuel.

"Let's take a break from the family for a few minutes."

"Okay." *Thank goodness.* She hadn't wanted to say anything. Everyone was being so very kind. It was just such a big family. She was a little overwhelmed.

He took her hand and pulled her into a hug. "Are you happy?"

"Of course." She pulled back and his lips went to hers.

"Let's sit." He nudged her toward the sofa.

She turned to sit and stopped. Her thoughts froze. There was a teddy bear there on the sofa. A teddy bear that looked like Pappa, the one Samuel had given her.

In her fit of anger, she'd left him at her apartment here in Houston. She'd called the movers and the apartment office, but no one had seen him. She'd kicked herself a hundred times for leaving him behind in anger.

Maybe everyone in the family had one of them.

She sat next to the teddy bear and couldn't resist picking it up. "This looks like…"

The bear had a pink ribbon tied around its neck. "Pappa."

She ran her hand along the ribbon that was looped through a ring. She lifted the ring. It was a glittery diamond.

"Samuel," She turned, the bear in her hands. "Is this…?"

He was on his knees with a grin on his face. "Pappa and I have something to ask you."

She held her breath.

"Danielle." He took her hands. She inhaled raggedly.

"Is this my bear?"

"Yes. It's your bear. Your bear and I want to ask you something."

"Okay."

He squeezed the bear's paw. And the words "Will you marry me?" came from the bear.

He slipped the ribbon off the bear and held up the ring. "Will you marry me?"

"Yes," she breathed, going into his arms and into a kiss.

After a few minutes, she asked. "How did you get Pappa? I thought he was lost."

"I went to your apartment the day you moved out. The movers told me you'd left. I couldn't just leave him."

"Samuel, I called everybody looking for him."

"Then I'm glad I rescued him."

"I am too." She got off of the floor and sat on the sofa, pulling him with her. She pressed the bear's paw and giggled. Pappa had learned to talk. Then, with her expression serious again, she turned back to Samuel. "Are you sure? You're taking on some serious baggage."

"Hey. I knew about the baggage before you did. Surely that counts for something."

"True. I'm not sure what that says about me."

"I think it means we're an awesome pair."

"We do work well together."

"I was thinking more like we play well together."

She flushed. "We play well together, too."

"So," he said, "since you said yes, I don't have to help you slink out the back door. Everyone's waiting out there."

"They knew?"

"Don't even try keeping something like this from my family. All it takes is for one person to have a suspicion, and suddenly everyone is all over it. I think they have cake."

She laughed. "Then let's not keep them waiting."

And together, they went out to announce their engagement to his family.

63

*W*ith family living in Alabama, Texas, and California, and two pilots in the family, choosing a wedding location hadn't been easy.

It was Samuel's younger sister who first suggested a destination wedding. "Danielle's dad can fly us anywhere. Why wouldn't we take advantage of that? I, for one, wouldn't mind getting away for a few days."

Mrs. Johnson admonished her daughter for bringing it up, but the idea took on a life of its own and Savannah said almost the same exact words as Samuel's sister.

Savannah and Noah voted for the mountains in Colorado. Samuel's siblings wanted New Orleans. Samuel and Danielle were thinking a warm Florida beach.

But when Claire's doctor restricted her from flight travel, they went with the Long Beach Museum of Art with its beautiful view of the ocean at sunset.

The wedding was outside on a perfect April afternoon. It was a family-only affair. Nonetheless, her mother hadn't been able to resist small details like a white carpet for her to walk down the aisle on and rose petals scattered everywhere.

Samuel, Noah, and Grayson all wore tuxes – Danielle's soon-to-be husband, her father, and her stepfather. Danielle smiled at the sight of the handsome men in her family.

As they waited for their cue to walk down the aisle, Noah pulled Danielle aside. "Danielle. You know you don't have to do this. Between me and Savannah and your mother and Grayson, we'll help you raise the child. You'll have plenty of help."

"I'm not worried about that, Dad."

"We can stop now. It isn't too late."

"I thought you liked Samuel."

"I do like Samuel, but I want you to be sure. Not to feel like this is a train you can't stop."

"You couldn't pull me off this train if you tried."

Her father kissed her on the cheek. "Okay then. If he ever hurts you, you tell me, and I'll take care of it."

"Dad." She laughed. "I love Samuel. I *want* to marry him."

"Is everything good?" Grayson asked as they came back to stand in their places.

"Everything's perfect." Danielle hugged her stepfather.

Samuel stood waiting as her two fathers walked her down the aisle – one on each arm.

Danielle wore white – an empire A-Line floor-length wedding gown. It was sleeveless, but the skirt had mounds of tulle with layers and beading. She didn't hide her pregnancy, but she didn't accent it either. Unless she placed a hand beneath her stomach, it wasn't evident. For *something blue,* she wore flat Superga sneakers in blue. For something old, she wore a diamond necklace that her grandmother gave her, and for something borrowed, she wore a little homemade ring that her father had made for Savannah in college, but never had the chance to give to her.

When they reached the front of the aisle to stand in front of the priest, Danielle stood next to Samuel and the rest of the world faded away.

He had become so very dear to her. The way his lips curved up at the corners when he looked at her. His eyes that focused on her and only on her. The way their hands seemed to magnetically snap together when they were close.

Then there was the way he seemed in-tune to the nuances of her mood and to know her every need before even she did.

She was only content when he was near. She could no longer imagine a day without him in it.

When he said "I do," he said the words softly, only for her, leaning forward with his lips almost touching her cheek.

Then when the priest paused and looked at her, she said "I do" before he even said the words. It didn't matter what he said, what the words were. She wanted this man for the rest of her life.

Then Samuel leaned her back, Hollywood-style, and kissed her. Though she instinctively put her arms around his neck, his arms around her back were strong, holding her secure. Seconds ticked.

It wasn't until everyone started clapping that he set her back on her feet and grinned at her.

And just like that, she was Mrs. Samuel Johnson.

64

*D*anielle woke Samuel in the middle of the night. At first, he thought he was dreaming. "Samuel?"

"Samuel." She shook him this time.

He sat up in the bed, his heart racing. "What?"

"It's time."

She was already sitting up.

"Now?"

"Now."

"I need to send your mother a text." That was the plan, he'd send a text to her mother, and she would start the chain reaction that would send everyone to meet them at the hospital.

"I sent it already."

"Oh no! You can't take my job. Your mother will hate me."

She smiled smugly. "I sent it from your phone, silly."

"We should go then."

"Probably."

How was she so calm? Her father and Savannah were staying in a hotel not far from here and on the way to the hospital. Claire and Grayson were on standby. Samuel's family would come out later after they were settled in with the new baby.

Samuel got dressed, brushed his teeth, and helped Danielle from the bed. "Do you want me to carry you?"

"We'd both be on the floor. I can walk."

Their overnight bags were already in the car. He just had to grab their cell phones, wallet, and keys, and they were good to go.

It was all too simple.

Halfway to the car, the contractions hit her again. Danielle went to her knees in pain. Samuel, helpless to do anything other than comfort her, waited until she could walk again.

Another wave hit her in the car. Samuel drove faster.

When he got to the ER, everyone was already there. Noah met them at the car and helped Samuel get Danielle out and to the door.

Someone showed up with a wheelchair.

Samuel wheeled her inside.

Everything for the next three hours was a blur.

The only thing that Samuel remembered clearly was when the doctor put the squirming little baby in Samuel's arms. He sat on the bed next to Danielle and gingerly placed the baby in her mother's arms. Danielle smiled up at him.

It was in that moment that Samuel knew that from this moment forward, he would think of the baby as his. It didn't matter that she wasn't his biologically. He and Danielle had brought this baby into the world together. They would raise it together and love it together.

"Have you decided?" They had talked about so many different names. They had finally decided that they would know when the baby got here.

Danielle looked down at the cooing infant. "Samantha Skye."

Samuel beamed. His first choice. Samantha after him, and

Skye just because it was such an awesomely fitting name for the daughter and granddaughter of a pilot.

Samuel bent over and kissed her on the tip of the nose. "I love it. And I love you."

65

*D*anielle felt like she'd been through hell and back.

But it didn't matter. She had a beautiful baby girl to show for it, and Samuel was going to be the most awesome father.

Her heart warmed as he placed the baby carefully in her arms.

"Before I bring in the rest of the family, I'd like to ask you something."

"Okay." She took a deep breath. "But keep in mind, I may not be exactly coherent."

"That's kind of what I wanted to talk about."

She waited. Was this where he told her this was more than he could handle?

"Was it so terrible? Having a baby?" He reached and smoothed her damp hair.

"It was awful and wonderful all at the same time."

"But look what we have to show for it."

"She's beautiful." Danielle put the baby's tiny little hand in hers and counted her fingers. Again.

"So… I was thinking."

"Oh boy."

He laughed. "I was wondering how you felt about thinking – just thinking – about us making one of these little guys together."

"I've been thinking about that for quite some time, actually." She smiled into his eyes.

"So have I. But not just the process. Once you're over your pregnancy, but to have one to go with this one."

"That's something I'm willing to take into consideration."

He took her hand and kissed her fingers. "But then if you decide you never want to go through this again, I totally wouldn't blame you."

"I totally want to give little Samantha a little brother or sister."

"I never want to tell her."

Her heart stuttered a little. "You never want to tell Samantha?" She rocked the sleeping baby gently.

"I want to be her father. I never want her to doubt that I chose her. I don't want her to know about the... sperm donor."

"Deal." Danielle had been thinking similarly. "It may come up again, but I won't bring it up."

He pressed his lips against hers. Her eyes fluttered closed.

Today was her daughter's birthday.

And the man of her dreams was here next to her.

Maybe happily ever after wasn't just a myth after all.

EPILOGUE

$\mathcal{D}$anielle straightened her skirt and slipped into her heels. Today was her daughter's birthday. She was one-year-old today.

And in about one hour, her house would be filled with family.

She and Samuel were waiting a bit to start on baby number two. Right now, their hands were more than full with little Samantha. She was a good baby, but with both of them doting on her, she took most of their time.

Neither one of them had been apart from her at night yet.

They were working on that.

In fact, tonight, after the baby's party, she and Samuel had reservations at an Italian restaurant down the street.

With Danielle's family there, they had agreed that it was the perfect time for Danielle and Samuel to have their first post-baby date.

She peeked out the back window where Samuel was busy with the grill. Samantha played at her feet. She scooped the baby up and went downstairs to the kitchen.

There was nothing left to do. The cake was ready. The gifts were wrapped.

When the doorbell rang, she knew it would be her mother and Grayson before she even looked. She hugged both of them, and Grayson took Samantha.

In his other hand, Grayson carried little Beau – named after Claire's maiden name Beauchamp - in a little baby carrier.

Danielle and Claire had no more than gotten to the kitchen when the doorbell rang. It was her father and his wife Savannah.

Samuel came in through the back door and took it in stride that everyone was an hour early.

"We're a little early," Noah said.

"I couldn't keep him away." Savannah said reaching for the baby, Samantha.

"Who couldn't keep who away?" Noah said.

"It's great," Samuel grinned. "Let me just wash up, and I'll get you all something to drink."

"I'll help you." Grayson shrugged when Claire rolled her eyes.

"He gets a little nervous when there are too many babies around."

"I do not."

"Since everyone's here," Danielle said, "there's no reason why we can't go ahead and get the babies ready for the party."

"Sounds like a great idea." Savannah agreed.

Claire set down her diaper bag. "I couldn't agree more. Then the babies can take a nap while we rest and have a glass of wine. I'm exhausted."

Savannah nodded. "Danielle, you did it right. Don't wait until you're our age to have a baby. If you think you're tired now, just imagine having twenty years on you."

"At least you know what you're doing."

Both Savannah and Claire laughed. "If only."

"Sounds like our cue to head out to the barbecue pit." Noah said.

"Men." Both women said at the same time.

Danielle followed Samuel into the kitchen and put wine glasses on a tray while he washed up.

"It's kind of amazing that your divorced parents get along so well."

"It is, isn't it? My mom and dad had sort of an arranged marriage. And now both of them are back with their high school sweethearts."

"I hope you don't get any ideas like that."

Danielle handed him the bottle of wine and the corkscrew. "Not a chance. You're stuck with me."

"I'm just glad we don't have to deal with Joey."

"I know. I haven't heard from him since the letter."

"I don't think he'll bother us."

Danielle laughed. "Me either. I don't know what you said to him that night at my apartment in Houston, but he's staying away."

Samuel shrugged. "I'll never tell."

"We should probably leave the wine in here until the babies go to sleep."

He chuckled. "That's probably a good idea."

Danielle carried the birthday cake, and Samuel carried the plates and forks.

"If we're doing the cake now, I'll have to get the guys back inside," Savannah said.

"I think we should do it while the babies are still awake." Claire pointed out.

They set up the dining room table while Savannah got Noah and Grayson back inside. Then they rounded up the babies, and, after putting little Samantha in her high chair, both Savannah and Claire sat with their babies in their laps.

They sang *Happy Birthday*, passed out cake, which soon

went everywhere, and Danielle helped Samantha open her presents – practical nonslip socks from Grayson, a fly and learn airplane from Noah, a little red wagon from Claire, a Manhattan treetop adventure activity center from Savannah, and a sit-to-stand walker from Mom and Dad.

An hour later, the house looked like a tornado went through it, but the babies were all three asleep.

Savannah collapsed on the sofa. "We need wine."

"And we need to get the barbeque going." Noah suggested.

"We have that taken care of." Danielle said.

Samuel poured wine for everyone, but poured sparkling water in his own glass.

"What's up?" Danielle leaned over and asked.

"Someone has to be a designated driver. With three infants in the house, you never know. Besides, I'm driving to the restaurant."

"Good point. I'll have water, too."

ANOTHER EPILOGUE

"Um Samuel." Danielle looked up from her phone. "I think you missed the turn to the restaurant."

"I'm taking the scenic route." He winked at her, and she went back to her phone.

"We got some really good pictures of Samantha. I'm sending some of them to your family."

"Thanks, love."

A few minutes later, Danielle looked up again. "Where are we going?"

"The airport."

She frowned at him. "Why? We're going to miss our reservation."

"I think we're going to just make it."

She answered a text on her phone. "You're acting strange."

"I know. I told your dad I wouldn't be able to pull it off."

She groaned. "Oh no. What did my dad talk you into?"

"Actually it was my idea. He just helped with the details."

"Are we flying somewhere?"

"Yes." Samuel beamed at her. "But I'm not supposed to tell you. It's supposed to be a surprise."

She almost pressured him into telling her. It wouldn't take much effort. But instead, she decided to go along and let him surprise her.

Besides, it was kind of fun wondering what he had planned. With Savannah and Claire at their house, she felt safe leaving Samantha there under their watch.

And… she could peek at the Nest cams at any time.

She leaned her head back against the seat and rested her eyes until they got to the airport.

They climbed into his little Mooney airplane, and she watched as he prepared to fly. She loved it when he went into pilot mode. Other women may find firemen attractive or even doctors, but for Danielle, it was pilots— or maybe just one pilot in particular.

An hour later, they were flying over the Magic Kingdom at Disneyland. Danielle beamed at her husband as their wheels touched down at John Wayne Airport.

After he turned off the plane and helped her down, he said. "I seem to recall that on the day we met, you told me that your perfect birthday would be to have dinner at the Magic Kingdom castle. Since we couldn't go on your birthday, I thought our daughter's birthday would be the next best thing."

She put her arms around him. "It isn't the next best thing." She kissed him on the lips. "It's perfect."

How about a free short story?

GET MY BONUS SHORT STORY
https://BookHip.com/JCARAKF

Read the next sweet story in the Worthingtons Series.

Turn the page for a preview of Just Stay…

JUST STAY PREVIEW

CHAPTER 1

*J*sobel LaFleur adjusted her sunglasses. The bright Dallas sun coming in through the windshield of the little Cessna Citation, one of Noah Worthington's newest private jets, was brutal.

She was just back from a quick turnaround flight to Denver. Dropping off a woman and her Australian shepherd for a visit to her daughter's house.

Isobel had spent some time vacuuming up the dog hair and wiping down the windows and seat. Dogs invariably drooled on windows. Every time.

As she went down her pre-flight checklist, she absently swept away a floating dog hair. There would be dog hairs in the cabin for days.

Otherwise, it was a light day for her, especially for a Friday, and she had a long weekend ahead.

She had to take a passenger - she glanced at her clipboard - Matthew Rodgers - to a small town in Louisiana, then fly him back to Dallas on Sunday.

The drive to Marigold, Louisiana wasn't more than four hours at the most by car, but to each his own. Besides, those who preferred the convenience of flying over driving paid the rent.

The biggest problem was that Isobel was from a small town just north of Houston. She'd worked hard to get out of there, vowing to herself that she'd never live in a small town again.

So the prospect of spending two nights in a town so small she'd never even heard of it was off-putting to say the least.

But taking care of clients was Noah Worthington's first and foremost policy. He'd built Skye Travels out of nothing more than a dream and now landing a job flying for him was more coveted than flying for any of the major airlines.

Isobel had been with Skye Travels for about eighteen months now. And the job so far had lived up to her expectations and then some.

She absolutely loved it. She could pretty much set her own schedule, within reason, of course. She could request short out and back day trips or she could ask for longer trips.

That particular perk of the job - reasonable freedom - came with a give and take.

When a flight like the one she was on today came up all of a sudden - as so many of them did - Noah looked for volunteers.

Isobel hadn't had anything on her schedule for the weekend. And to be honest, flying was flying, even if it did involve spending two nights in a little town in Louisiana.

And it got her out of her best friend's wedding dress try on thing. She'd already done two of them. And sitting in a wedding dress shop while her friend came out in various dresses wasn't all that exciting. The most exciting part was holding up little hand-painted signs that read things like *Love it* or *Next* or *No Way.*

But the whole process would take the better part of half a day and, though Isobel had a high tolerance for boredom, she found waiting for her friend to change from dress to dress interminable.

Isobel was excited for her friend, but her personal idea of a romantic wedding involved a flight to Vegas.

She didn't get into the whole tradition of trying on a million wedding dresses and tasting wedding cakes and... monogramed cookies, for God's sake.

And, of course, with the whole Vegas option, there was flying involved.

Matthew Rodgers was late.

With the way commercial airlines had people trained to be early, it was unusual for a passenger to actually be late for his flight.

She thought about calling him. She had his phone number right there on her clipboard.

But decided instead to use the time to help Gretta sort through some dresses.

Gretta had found a cool app that she and all her friends could log into. They'd swipe right if they liked a dress or left if they didn't.

After everyone went through the dresses, Gretta would be able to see which dresses her friends thought would be best for her. It was supposed to cut down on the trying on and modeling part of the process, but Isobel doubted that would actually happen. Gretta enjoyed trying on dresses way too much.

Isobel started swiping. Then stopped and sent Gretta a quick text. *Really... I can fly you two to Vegas.*

She got a quick message back. A cute emoji of Gretta shaking her gorgeous head of long blonde hair.

Ah well. It was worth a try. It wasn't the first time she'd offered and it wouldn't be the last. The wedding wasn't until December, so she had at least six months to change Gretta's mind.

Ten minutes later a limo pulled out on the tarmac and stopped near her plane.

Isobel tamped down her negative thoughts about the entitled rich and put a smile on her face. Just because he drove up in a limo... and was late... didn't make him a bad person.

She went to the door of the plane and waited for the driver to unload Matthew's luggage onto a cart. A baggage handler then loaded the passenger's luggage - three big suitcases and a trunk - alongside her one suitcase.

She was reminded of a trip she and Gretta had taken together. It had been the one time Isobel and Gretta had gone on a cruise. Gretta had taken practically every outfit she owned, making Isobel look like a pauper next to her.

Gretta had loved the cruise. The whole dressing up - a different outfit for every activity. Isobel had been in hell. She would have left after the first day. But of course, that wasn't an option.

After that, Isobel hadn't taken any more trips where she didn't have access to either a car or an airplane.

The driver opened the passenger's door and after a few minutes a man with a set of crutches stepped out.

That explained a lot. She'd never been on crutches herself, but it made sense that everything took longer to do.

The man who stepped out of the limo and took the crutches had to be Matthew.

He wore a cast on the bottom half of his left leg.

A blue baseball cap on his head plastered with a large T and dark sunshades hid most of his appearance. But he was tall with a lean muscular build. He was wearing a tee-shirt and gray jogging pants. Quite comfortably dressed for the short flight. Most of her passengers flew at least in their Sunday best. But then most passengers weren't wearing a cast.

Isobel went back to the cockpit and waited. She didn't want to stare as Matthew laboriously made his way to the plane.

It took a bit of maneuvering, but after handing his crutches to the driver, he climbed aboard.

Isobel adjusted the black captain's hat that was part of her uniform and came out to greet her passenger.

"Hello," she said with a bright smile. "I'm Isobel LaFleur. I'll be your pilot today."

Matthew didn't even look at her. He frowned as he adjusted his leg and removed his sunshades. His eyes, flickering in her direction for only a second, were the bluest blue Isobel had ever seen.

"Then we should get going, don't you think?"

"Of course." Isobel kept the smile on her lips, but it faded from her eyes.

She took her seat and began going down the pre-flight checklist.

He was the one who'd been late.

She'd been quite patient waiting on him.

And now he wanted to *get going.*

Isobel would get going alright. She knew how to be professional but distant.

Matthew Rodgers better hope he didn't need anything extra.

CHAPTER 2

Matthew Rodgers was in hell.

Going anywhere. Doing anything was an ordeal. Even sitting here on the little airplane.

Since he couldn't drive, his little sports car sat in storage for who knew how many weeks.

He'd torn his calf muscle completely in half. And besides the pain in the neck of using crutches, the pain that radiated through his calf was almost unendurable at times.

He took a sip of the clear seltzer water the pilot had

provided. He hadn't had any special requests. But the girl on the phone at Skye Travels kept asking.

So he just made up something. He didn't even like seltzer water. Plain old tap water suited him just fine.

He would have stayed home through all this if he'd had a choice, but when he made a commitment, he did everything he could to follow through.

And he wasn't about to subject any of his friends to a weekend with his family. Or vice versa.

And right now, the Rangers were willing to pay for whatever it took to keep him happy.

It wasn't even their fault. He'd been standing on the field during baseball practice, sure, but it could have happened anywhere.

He'd simply taken a step backwards and his calf muscle had popped, leaving it torn completely in two.

That kind of thing normally happened when an athlete was doing something athletic. Not taking a step backwards.

The doctors called it a freak accident.

Matthew could have used a little less freakiness in his life.

The pilot was pretty and she seemed sweet.

He just wasn't in the mood for pretty or sweet.

Besides, being a pilot, she'd also be smart. And Matthew hadn't been around that many smart women lately.

He wasn't sure he had the energy right now to keep up his end of a meaningful conversation.

He just wanted to get this weekend over with and get back to his apartment.

Then he could stew in his misfortune. Alone.

But he only had one little sister and she was getting engaged.

He needed to meet the guy before all this went too far along the path.

If he was honest with himself, he had to admit that it was

already too far gone or they wouldn't be having this engagement party.

That's what happened when he put his career first.

Family slid into second place and little sisters got engaged.

The flight was smooth.

And he promised himself he'd be nice as the wheels touched down on the little runway in Marigold, Louisiana.

The airport was out in the middle of nowhere. A wide-open space surrounded by trees on all sides. Just one opening for a little blacktop road that led to the highway.

It would be okay. He wouldn't be here long.

A visit didn't mean he would be stuck here. He'd gotten away from the small town and a visit didn't mean anything more than a visit.

If he could just talk his sister into moving to the city...

The plane came to a stop and after a few minutes, the pilot opened the door.

The smile she'd had for him earlier was gone. In its stead was a serious professionalism. He'd caused that.

"Do you need any help getting out?" she asked.

Matthew shook his head. "Nah. I can manage." He maneuvered himself out of the plane and stood on his crutches.

The doctors had been smart. They'd arranged the cast so that he couldn't put any weight on his leg.

Still, every little movement hurt like hell.

Isobel looked around at the little runway that passed for an airport. No other planes. No cars.

Nothing.

"Um. Do we need to call anyone?" she asked.

Matthew pulled his phone out. "My brother's supposed to be here." He sent a quick text. Drake was always late.

Though Matthew had previously prided himself on being on time, this leg injury was pulling him into the family trait of being late.

"I can unload the luggage." Isobel seemed a bit unsure of how to proceed. Matthew got the feeling that she wasn't comfortable with the little runway. He wondered if she'd ever been to an airport this small.

An airport that was only a runway. Still it had a designation. ML1.

A text came in from Drake. *Ten minutes out.*

Matthew shot back. *Don't text and drive.*

Just answering your question.

Matthew blew out a breath. It was going to be a long weekend.

"Please don't," he said. "My brother will be here shortly."

Just minutes later an ancient green pickup truck came lumbering out of the trees toward the runway. Matthew heard the truck before he even saw it.

It was just like his brother to pick him up in the family's forty plus year-old beat up truck.

Drake loved to make fun of the fact that Matthew lived in the city in what he called a fancy apartment with regular cleaning service that took care of his house cleaning, laundry, etc.

Something only a brother could get away with.

Drake stepped out of the truck. His tall, lean body wearing faded jeans and a plaid flannel shirt.

Drake was really playing it to the hilt.

Matthew took a step forward, then stood there balancing on his crutches.

Drake took one look at Isobel and broke into a wide grin.

Isobel stood warily watching the two of them. She was slim and petite. Not more than five four or so. Her sleek brunette hair was pulled back in a ponytail beneath her captain's cap.

A few strands of hair had escaped the ponytail and fell about her face. She absently swept the hair away, keeping her attention on his brother.

Drake held out a hand. "Welcome to Marigold," he said. "My name's Drake."

Matthew had to bite his tongue.

He had, after all, seen her first.

Keep Reading Just Stay...

Kathryn Kaleigh is the author of over seventy novels, over one hundred short stories, and many collections.

kathrynkaleigh.com